"ONE OF THE GREAT SERIES IN THE HISTORY OF THE AMERICAN DETECTIVE STORY!" —*New York Times*

Stunning Praise for Robert B. Parke

"ASTONISHES THE READER WI
PROBES BENEATH THE SURFAC
FAILS TO ENTERTAIN." —*New Yo*

"A FAST-MOVING STORY!" —*Hou*

"TERSE, HILARIOUS . . . INTENSELY ARRESTING."
—*Minneapolis Star & Tribune*

"THE LATEST SPENSER SAGA DELIVERS THE GOODS . . . IT'S LIKE SLIPPING INTO A FAVORITE RUMPLED TRENCHCOAT."
—*Boston Herald*

"VINTAGE PARKER!"
—*Ocala Star-Banner*

PRAISE FOR ROBERT B. PARKER AND SPENSER . . .

"THEY JUST DON'T MAKE PRIVATE EYES TOUGHER OR FUNNIER." —*People*

"PARKER'S DIALOGUE CRACKLES, AND HIS ONE-LINERS ARE AMONG THE BEST IN THE BUSINESS." —*Washington Post*

"SPENSER IS THE SASSIEST, FUNNIEST, MOST-ENJOYABLE-TO-READ-ABOUT PRIVATE EYE AROUND TODAY!"
—*Cincinnati Post*

"ROBERT B. PARKER HAS TAKEN HIS PLACE BESIDE DASHIELL HAMMETT, RAYMOND CHANDLER, AND ROSS MACDONALD." —*Boston Globe*

"SPENSER. HE'S HOT." —*Tacoma Sun*

Don't miss Spenser's previous thriller . . .

PLAYMATES

"THE BEST SPENSER MYSTERY NOVEL IN MANY A YEAR." —*New York Times*

"A WHOLE LOTTA FUN . . . READERS CAN KICK BACK AND ENJOY!"
—New York *Daily News*

"*PLAYMATES* IS A SUCCESS . . . THE DIALOGUE IS SALTY AND THE ACTION SWIFT." —*Boston Globe*

Continued . . .

More praise for Robert B. Parker

"READING PARKER IS LIKE SWIMMING DOWNSTREAM IN A RIVER OF ADRENALINE!"
—*Boston Observer*

"THE LEGITIMATE HEIR TO THE HAMMETT-CHANDLER-MACDONALD TRADITION."
—*Cincinnati Post*

"WHAT A FIND ROBERT PARKER IS!"
—*Los Angeles Times*

"SPENSER GIVES THE TRIBE OF HARD-BOILED WONDERS A NEW VITALITY AND COMPLEXITY."
—*Chicago Sun-Times*

"ONE OF THE MOST ENGAGING CHARACTERS IN CONTEMPORARY AMERICAN FICTION. Parker writes exciting, genuinely witty stories populated by wacky characters . . . Delightful."
—*Grand Rapids Press*

"ROBERT PARKER IS STILL TOP GUN IN THE TOUGH-GUY SCHOOL OF FICTION."
—*Playboy*

"SPENSER IS A CONSTANT REVELATION FOR EVEN LONGTIME PARKER FANS."
—*Milwaukee Sentinel*

and SPENSER . . .

"SPENSER IS BOSTON'S ANSWER TO JAMES BOND, with a little Sam Spade and Nero Wolfe thrown in . . . IRREVERENT, WITTY, AND WORLDLY." —*Pittsburgh Press*

SPENSER IS "AS TOUGH AS THEY COME AND SPIKED WITH A TOUCH OF REAL CLASS."
—*Kirkus*

"THE BEST PRIVATE EYE IN FICTION SINCE RAYMOND CHANDLER."
—*Dan Wakefield*

"PARKER'S SPECIALTIES ARE ACTION, HUMOR, AND ATMOSPHERE . . . LADLED OUT IN GENEROUS DOSES."
—*New York Times*

SPENSER IS "TOUGHER, STRONGER, BETTER EDUCATED, AND FAR MORE AMUSING THAN SAM SPADE, PHIL MARLOWE, OR LEWIS ARCHER." —*Boston Globe*

"THE VERY BEST OF THE BREED!"
—*Providence Journal*

"PARKER HAS PERFECTED A GREAT FORMULA . . . HIS MYSTERIES HIT ALL THE RIGHT BUTTONS!" —*Seattle Times*

"A SERIES THAT IS SPLENDID!"
—*Fort Worth Star-Telegram*

Other books by Robert B. Parker

POODLE SPRINGS (with Raymond Chandler)
PLAYMATES
CRIMSON JOY
PALE KINGS AND PRINCES
TAMING A SEA-HORSE
A CATSKILL EAGLE
VALEDICTION
LOVE AND GLORY
THE WIDENING GYRE
CEREMONY
A SAVAGE PLACE
EARLY AUTUMN
LOOKING FOR RACHEL WALLACE
WILDERNESS
THE JUDAS GOAT
THREE WEEKS IN SPRING (with Joan Parker)
PROMISED LAND
MORTAL STAKES
GOD SAVE THE CHILD
THE GODWULF MANUSCRIPT

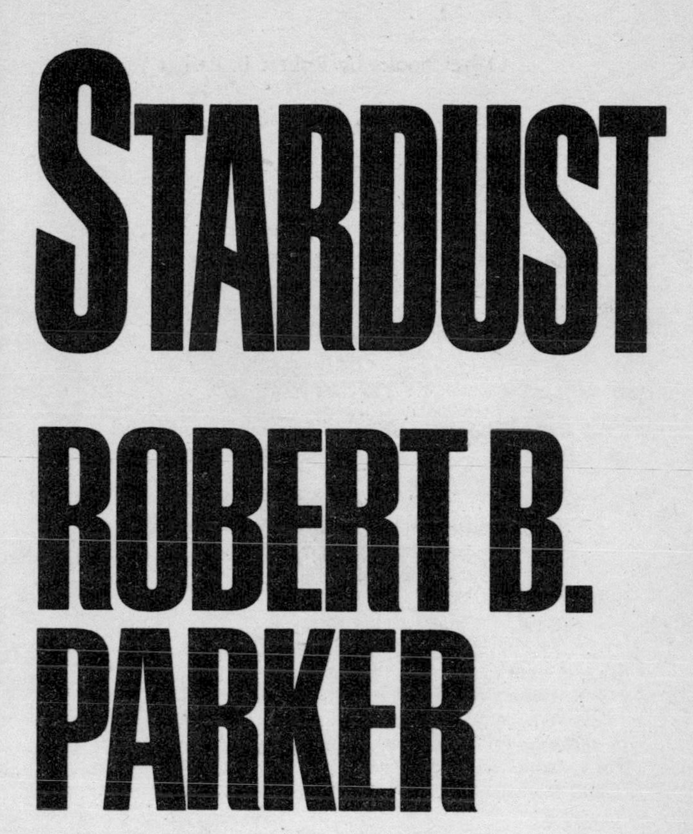

BERKLEY BOOKS, NEW YORK

This Berkley book contains the complete text
of the original hardcover edition. It has been
completely reset in a typeface designed for easy
reading and was printed from new film.

STARDUST

A Berkley Book / published by arrangement with
the author

PRINTING HISTORY
G. P. Putnam's Sons edition / June 1990
Published simultaneously in Canada
Berkley edition / May 1991

ISBN: 0-425-12723-0

A BERKLEY BOOK® TM 757,375
Berkley Books are published by The Berkley Publishing Group,
200 Madison Avenue, New York, New York 10016.

PRINTED IN THE UNITED STATES OF AMERICA

10 9 8 7 6 5 4 3 2 1

STARDUST

1

WHEN you walk across the Common from the Beacon Street side, coming up from Charles Street and angling toward Park Street, you are walking up one of those low urban hills that no one notices, unless they are running. At the top, with the State House at about ten o'clock and the Park Street Church straight ahead at twelve o'clock high, you look down toward the Park Street Station. Which is what Susan and I were doing on an early winter day, with maybe three inches of old snow on the ground, and the temperature about seventeen. Below us, at the corner of Park and Tremont, the big subway kiosk was surrounded by trailers and trucks and mysterious equipment. Thick cables ran into the subway entrance, maybe two hundred people bustled about in various kinds of arctic wear. There were big yellow trucks with Hertz-Penske lettered on the sides. There were long trailers with many small doors.

"It looks like Hertz-Penske is invading Park Street Under," I said.

Susan nodded. Her nose was slightly red from the cold and her gloved hand was firm in mine.

"Show business," she said. "Can you smell the grease paint?"

"That's my shaving lotion," I said. "Besides, I don't think they use grease paint in television."

"It's just an expression," Susan said. "Have you no feeling for the romance of the theater?"

"Sure," I said. "Sure I do."

We walked down the hill toward the film site. The snow was crisp, and dry as sand in the cold. The trees around the Common were black and angular with hard snow in the places where the big limbs branched out. The fountain, where in summer the bums reclined, glaring at the tourists, was still and icy, and people cutting across the Common for a late breakfast meeting at the Ritz or the Four Seasons were hunch-shouldered, high-collared, hurrying stiffly through the chill. I had on a black Navy watch cap and a leather jacket with the fleece lining zipped in, and my gun in a shoulder holster under my left arm, to keep the bullets warm.

Inside the kiosk the stairs ran down steeply to the station. An escalator ran parallel to the stairs and the hot industrial smell of the subway system rose to meet us as we went through the door. The camera and light cables ran down along the sides of the stairs and a couple of MBTA cops were there to steer the subway customers past them. The station was still fully functioning, and the filming worked around that fact. Mixed among the customers was a squadron of technicians, each a mismatched ode to Eddie Bauer in down parka and insulated moon boots.

"Used to have those in Korea," I said to Susan.

"Called them Mickey Mouse boots. They were a little less colorful, but just as ugly."

At the foot of the stairs to the left of the turnstiles, a small area was brightly lit with the big movie lights that you always see in ads. A couple of high-backed black canvas chairs stood just outside the lighted circle. On the back in white script was written, *Fifty Minutes.* There were cameramen and lighting men and sound men with earphones. There were assistant directors to herd the civilians around the shooting area, and a first assistant with the script in a big leather holster. A guy wearing a hat that looked like a World War I aviator's helmet, with the straps undone and the earpieces flapping, was setting up the shot; and there in the middle of the bright area wearing a tight red dress and a black mink coat thrown over her shoulders was Jill Joyce, America's honeybun.

Susan nudged me. I nodded.

Jill Joyce said, "Harry, for crissake, how long are you going to fuck around with this shot?"

"Pretty soon, Jilly," the guy with the earflaps said. "I want you to look just about perfect, Jilly." Harry was looking through a lens he wore on a string around his neck and he spoke to Jill Joyce the way you speak to your puppy, in a kind of remote coddling tone that expects neither comprehension nor response. Jill Joyce waggled one of her hands toward a production assistant. He put a lighted cigarette in her hand. She took it without looking, dragged in a big lungful of smoke, and let it out in two streams through her nose.

Harry backed away a little, gazing through his lens, then he straightened and nodded. The first assistant director spoke into a bullhorn, "Quiet, please . . . rolling for picture." A red-haired woman with a thick sheaf of script open on a clipboard stepped in and took Jill's cigarette. Jill stared into the camera; her face got prettier. A little guy with a straggly beard and an orange down vest jumped into the shot with a clacker and clacked. Behind Jill the subway train that had been idling there patiently began to creep forward. ". . . and action," Harry yelled. Jill looked off camera right and called out, "Rick? It's all right, Rick, I'm here." Her eyes scanned past the camera, looking for Rick. The train pulled on through behind her and moved on down the tunnel. The camera panned after it as it went and held on, its taillights disappearing, and Harry said, "Cut. It's a keeper."

Jill put her hand out again in the general direction of the script person and waggled it. The script woman handed her the lighted cigarette and she took another big drag, dropped it on the floor, shrugged deeper into her mink, and headed toward the escalator. A uniformed Boston cop named Ray Morrissey walked ahead of Jill and moved people out of her way.

"Wow," I said. "Was that magic, or what?"

Susan grinned. "God save me, I could watch it all day."

"Really?" I said.

"You think I'm deeply disturbed?" Susan said.

"Yes," I said.

She nodded. "Yes," she said. "I think you're right." Then she smiled her smile that made Jill Joyce look like a cow flap and nodded her head toward a group standing beyond the escalator.

"There's Sandy," she said.

Sandy was state-of-the-art Eddie Bauer. He had on a full-length gold-colored down-lined jumpsuit, with black fur-topped thermal boots half zipped and a black knit ski cap with a large golden tassel. He was short and probably wiry but who could tell in the down jumpsuit. He had a goatee. With him was a hatless man with a lot of black curly hair, a strong nose, and dark skin. As we moved through the crowd toward them, the crew was packing up equipment, folding light stands, coiling cable, dismantling the cameras, packing up the sound gear. Everyone seemed to know what he was doing, which made this a unique enterprise in my experience.

Susan said, "Sandy."

Sandy turned and smiled at her. His glance took me in too, but it didn't harm the smile.

"Susan," Sandy said. "And this has got to be Mr. Spenser." Beyond Sandy and the guy with the black curly hair was a youngish guy with a round face and rimless glasses. He looked at both of us without expression.

Susan introduced me. "This is Sandy Salzman," she said. "He's the line producer." Susan had been consulting on the show for less than a month now and already she spoke a language as arcane as the psychological tech talk of which I'd but recently cured her. We shook hands.

"This is Milo Nogarian," Susan said, gesturing toward the guy with the curls, "the executive producer, and Marty Riggs, from Zenith." We shook hands.

"Susan is the consultant we hired, Marty," Sandy said. "And Mr. Spenser is a, ah, private security consultant, that maybe is going to give us a hand with Jill."

Marty Riggs gazed at me with his gray expressionless eyes, enlarged a bit by the rimless glasses. He was wearing a tweed cap and a cable-stitched white wool sweater under a thick Donegal tweed jacket with a long scarf wrapped around his neck. The loose ends of the scarf reached to his knees. He gave me a small stiff nod. I smiled warmly.

"Susan actually is a psychotherapist, Marty," Nogarian said. "Sees to it that we don't get our complexes mixed up." Susan smiled even more warmly than I had.

"I'm sure," Marty said. "Milo, just remember what I said. I don't want to have to go in to the network again and defend a piece of shit that you people have labeled script and sent over, *capice?*"

"Time, Marty," Nogarian said, "you know what the time pressures are like."

"And you know what cancellation is like, Milo. You have the top television star on the planet and you haven't broken the top ten yet, you know why? Script is why. Jill's been raising hell about them and she's right. I want something better, and I want to start seeing it tomorrow."

"How come your scarf's so long?" I said. Susan put her hand on my arm.

Riggs turned and looked at me. "What?" he said.

"Your scarf," I said, "is dangerously long. You might step on it and strangle yourself."

Susan dug her fingers into my arm.

"What the fuck are you talking about?" Riggs said.

"Your scarf. I may have to make a citizen's arrest here, your scarf is a safety hazard."

Riggs looked at Nogarian and Salzman. "Who the fuck is this guy, Milo?"

Nogarian looked as if he'd eaten something awful. Salzman seemed to be struggling with laughter. Susan's grip on my arm was so hard now that if I weren't tougher than six roofing nails it might have hurt.

"Looks dandy though," I said.

Whoever Riggs was he was used to getting more respect than I was giving him, and he couldn't quite figure out what to do about me.

"If you want to work around here, buddy," he said, "you better watch your step." Then he glared at all of us and turned and walked away. In a moment he was on the ascending escalator, and soon he had risen from sight.

Nogarian said, "Jesus Christ."

Salzman let out the laughter he'd been suppressing. "Wonderful," he said as he laughed, "a citizen's arrest. You gotta love it."

"Who is he, anyway?" I said.

"Senior VeePee," Salzman said, "Creative Affairs, One Hour, Zenith Meridien Television."

"Why'd you lean on him?" Nogarian said.

"He seemed something of a dork," I said.

Salzman laughed again. "You start leaning on every dork in the television business, you're going to be a busy man."

"So many dorks," I said, "so little time."

"It's not going to help us with the studio," Nogarian said.

"Milo, it was worth it," Salzman said, "watching Marty try to figure out who Spenser was so he could figure out if he should take shit from him or fire him." Salzman snorted with laughter. "You ready for some lunch?"

"Since breakfast," I said.

"Come on," Salzman said, and we followed him up the escalator. The subway station was empty of film crew. The equipment was gone, the cables had been stowed. It was as if they'd never been there.

As we went up the escalator Susan put her arm through mine. "I know why you needled Marty Riggs," she said.

"Sworn duty," I said, "as a member of the dork patrol."

"You needled him because he ignored me."

"That's one of the defining characteristics of a dork."

"Probably," Susan said.

We rode the rest of the way to the top, where the light, filtered through the glass, looked warmer than it was, and went out into the cold behind Salzman and Nogarian.

2

"I've got to have lunch with some people from the film commission," Nogarian said. "Sandy can fill you in on our situation." We shook hands and he headed down Winter Street toward Locke-Ober's.

"We're feeding in the basement over here near Tremont Temple," Salzman said. "I've asked Jill to join us."

We went across Tremont Street and in through a glass door into a corridor and down some stairs. At the bottom was a large basement room that looked as if it might be a recreational space for a boys' club or a church group. There was a serving counter set up along one side, and tables with folding chairs filled the room. The crew was spread out, down parkas hanging from chair backs, down vests tossed on the floor, hunched over trays eating. There was roast turkey with gravy, baked ham with pineapple, cold cuts, cheese, two kinds of tossed salad, succotash, mashed potatoes, green beans with bacon, and baked haddock with a cheese sauce. I noticed that the official crew meal was some of everything. Salzman had some ham and some haddock and a large helping of mashed potatoes. I was watching Susan. Her normal lunch was something like a lettuce leaf, dressing on the side. She carefully walked the length of the serving table and studied her options. I waited for her. When she was through she came back and picked up a tray.

"What do you think," I said.

"Eek," she said. She put plastic utensils on her tray and had a large serving of tossed salad with no dressing on a paper plate. I had some turkey.

Salzman had saved us a table in the corner, with space reserved for Jill Joyce when she arrived. Most of the tables seated twelve. This was the only small one.

"So what do you know about the deal here," Salzman said when we were seated.

"I know Susan's working for you as a technical adviser on this show, which is about a woman shrink and her husband who's a cop."

"Right," Salzman said. "You seen the show?"

"No," I said.

"Premise is ridiculous," Susan said.

"Right," I said. "How could a sophisticated psychotherapist fall for the kind of semi-thug that gets to be a cop?"

"Semi?" Susan said.

Salzman said, "Yeah, anyway. We got Jill Joyce to star. I assume I don't need to tell you about Jill Joyce."

"I know about the screen persona," I said. "Beautiful, wholesome, just kookie enough for a little wrinkled-nose fun?"

"Yeah," Salzman said. "She's a little different, in fact."

"Un huh."

"Anyway, she's been getting a series of harassing phone calls and things happening to her lately, and it's making her nervous. When Jill's nervous . . ." Salzman shrugged, raised his eyebrows, and shook his head slightly.

"What do you mean, sort of harassing?" I said.

"Hard to say exactly what it is. Jill's not too clear on it. She's clear that it's bothering her."

"And the things happening to her?" I said.

Salzman shrugged. "Things." He turned a palm up. "That's what Jill says, *things.*"

"Anybody else heard these calls or seen these *things?*"

Salzman shook his head. I looked at Susan. She shrugged.

"So Jill's, ah, demanding some action," Salzman said. "And Susan mentioned that she had a friend and one thing and another so I suggested you come over and have lunch and meet Jill. See if maybe you can help us out."

"Would I be working for you?" I said.

"Not technically."

"Who would I be working for technically?" I said.

"Michael J. Maschio," Sandy said.

"Who is?"

"President of Zenith Meridien Television, a subsidiary of Zenith Meridien Film Corporation."

"Not Riggs," I said.

"Hell, no, when Mike Maschio says *'green,'* Marty Riggs says, *'and a deep dark green it is, sir.'* "

Salzman ate some haddock.

"But actually," he said, "you'd be working for me."

He looked up and got to his feet.

"Here's Jill," he said.

I got to my feet. Jill Joyce, her black mink coat open, was swiveling through the dining room with Ray Morrissey a few feet back of her. Morrissey didn't look very happy. He looked at me and I shot him with my forefinger. He nodded once and when Jill reached us, peeled off without a word and headed for the chow line. Salzman was holding Jill's chair. She swivel-hipped around the table and sat in it and looked appraisingly at me from under her eyelids, slowly raising her head. Susan smiled and was quiet.

"Jill, you know Susan Silverman, our consultant. This is her friend that I mentioned to you, Mr. Spenser."

"Do you have a first name, Mr. Spenser?" Jill said. She had a soft girlish voice with just a hint of huskiness at the edges. I told her my first name.

"I don't like it," she said.

"I was afraid you wouldn't," I said. "I've been worried about it all month."

A small frown line deepened momentarily between her eyebrows and went away.

"I'll just make up a name for you," she said.

Susan's inward smile was widening. She said softly, "Boy, oh boy."

Jill stared at her coldly, and then turned back to me.

"What shall I call you," she said.

"Cuddles," I said. "Most of my closest friends call me that."

"Cuddles?"

"Yes," I said.

"You seem to have awfully big shoulders for *Cuddles.*"

Everything Jill Joyce said was said in a sort of half-childish lilt that implied sexual desire the way an alto sax implies jazz.

"Well," I said, "we'll think of something, I'm sure."

"Sandy says you're a dick," Jill Joyce said.

"Un hmm," I said with a straight face. Susan looked down at her salad.

"Are you going to help me, Dick?" she said. When she said *help* she leaned a little forward and let a hand flutter near her mouth. Tremulous.

"Sure," I said. "Tell me a little about what you need help with."

A dark-haired guy wearing a tee shirt and an apron came over with a tray. The tee shirt said *First Run Catering* on it. The tray carried a bottle of white wine in an ice bucket and a wineglass. The dark-haired guy put the tray down, opened the wine bottle, poured half a glass, waited while Jill sipped it. She nodded and he picked up the tray and departed.

Salzman said, "Jill, let me fix you a plate."

Jill smiled rather vaguely and nodded. Salzman

got up and headed for the serving line. Her eyes never left me. From the corner of my eye I saw Susan pick up a leaf of red-tipped lettuce, inspect it carefully, and take a neat little bite from one edge of it. Jill finished the half glass of wine and looked at me.

"May I pour you some?" I said.

"Oh, Dickie," she said, "how sweet."

I poured the white wine into her glass, waiting for her to say when or gesture with the rim that the glass was full enough. She did neither until I stopped because it was full. She drank about a third of it.

"So, Dickie," she said, "you're friends with, ah, this girl?" She made a sort of groping gesture with her left hand and finally nodded her head toward Susan.

"I'm friends with that girl," I said.

"Good friends?"

"Good friends."

"Sleep with her?"

"None of your business."

Susan was still nibbling on her greens, but she looked less amused. I knew how much she enjoyed being referred to in the third person. Almost as much as she liked being called a girl. I paused, giving her a moment to kneecap Jill Joyce. Nothing happened.

"Ohh, Dickie," Jill said with her lilt getting more pronounced. "No need to be snarky about it. A girl needs to know things."

"So does a dick," I said. "Tell me about these harassments you've been suffering."

Salzman came back with a dinner plate on which, carefully arranged, were small portions of nearly everything on the serving line. He put it down in front of Jill and slipped into his seat. Jill looked at the plate with distaste and drank more wine.

"I don't wish to discuss it in front of her," Jill said.

Susan looked at her quietly for a long moment.

"Oh boy, oh boy, oh boy," I said softly.

Then Susan smiled beatifically and said, "Of course."

"Of course?" I said.

"Please, Dick," Susan said.

She picked up her tray and moved over to another table and sat down with a couple of people at the end of a long table across the room.

"A girl has a right to privacy," Jill said, her eyes cast down on her untouched plate, her hand fluttering again near her mouth. I looked across the room at Susan. The force of her look was palpable. *Don't make trouble,* the look said. I took in a large amount of air and let it out slowly through my nose.

"So tell me," I said.

She looked at her empty wineglass. Salzman reached over and filled it.

"We got four and a half pages to shoot this afternoon, Jilly," he said.

"Fuck you," Jill Joyce said without looking at him. The lilt left her voice for a moment, when she said it.

Salzman nodded as if she had said something interesting. He leaned back in his chair and folded his arms quietly. He didn't seem upset. Jill drank some of her wine.

"I think it's one of those creepy crazed fans," she said and smiled at me. When she smiled there was a deep dimple in each cheek. She was something to look at.

"Un huh," I said and waited. I thought of steepling my hands before me and placing them gently against my lips when I said it, but decided to hold it in reserve. So far *un huh* seemed enough.

"Well," Jill said, "do you?"

"It's a little hard to decide yet," I said.

"But it could be," Jill said.

"Un huh."

"I mean, you know about these people, like the one that killed John Lennon, people like that, crazy people."

"Um," I said.

"I need prodection," she said.

"How clever," I said, "combining the words like that."

"Huh?"

"You need protection during production so you put the two together and formed a neologism."

"I don't know what the fuck you're talking about, Dickie-do, but I sure love to listen," she said. She didn't wait for anyone to fill her glass now; she poured the rest of the bottle out and looked around.

"Hey," she yelled toward the serving line. "I need some wine, for Christ's sake."

The same dark-haired guy in the tee shirt came

over with another bottle, already opened. He put it down beside her and walked back to the line. Most of the crew had started to leave the dining room. Susan had eaten enough of her lettuce. She stopped by at my table for a minute.

"I'll be in the wardrobe trailer . . . Dick."

I nodded. Susan moved off and out of the room. Sandy Salzman was gazing at the ceiling, his arms still folded across his chest.

"So you gonna protect me, Dickie-do? Or what?"

"Soon as I find out from what," I said, "I'm going to protect the ass off you."

Jill Joyce giggled.

"I'm sick of it here," she said. "Come on back to my mobile home and I'll dishcuss it with you in more detail."

"Sure," I said.

"Sandy, you go shoot some fucking film, or something. This will be just me and Dickie-bird." She giggled again. "Are you a dickie-bird?" she said.

Salzman smiled as if Jill had suggested a new approach to lighting.

"Sure, Jilly," Salzman said. "Maybe a little nap before the afternoon is gone. The four and a half pages await."

"Four and a half pages of shit," Jill said. "C'mon, Dickie-bird, we'll fly over to my mobile home."

She picked up the second wine bottle and her glass

and waggled on out of the dining room ahead of me. I looked at Salzman. He shrugged.

"No reasoning with her when she's drunk," Salzman said.

"Or when she's not," I said.

3

THE mobile home was parked on the Common behind the Park Street subway kiosk. It was big enough for Jill Joyce, or four hundred boat people. I wasn't sure it was big enough for Jill Joyce and me.

"Sit down, Dickie," she said.

She put her bottle of wine on the table in the breakfast nook and slid her black mink off her shoulders and let it fall to the floor. She slid in on one of the bench seats and let her long legs sprawl. The tight red dress was forced to hike up over her thighs.

"Want a little wine?" she said.

"Makes me sleepy," I said. "I drink at lunch and I'm no good the rest of the day."

"Wouldn't want that," Jill said.

She giggled and poured wine into a glass.

"You know what I've been looking for since I came to Boston?" she said.

"Two tickets to Symphony," I said.

She made a measuring gesture, holding her hands about two feet apart.

"About that long," she said. "I been looking for something about like that."

I studied her measure.

"Looks to be about two feet," I said.

She held her gesture, staring at me with her head canted back. Her eyes were narrowed. She jiggled her hands as if weighing the two-foot length.

I grinned and nodded. "You're in luck," I said.

Her eyes got narrower and something that looked only a little like a smile moved on her lips.

"You?" she said.

I shrugged becomingly.

"Unless I'm excited," I said.

The tip of her tongue appeared at the center of her mouth and moistened her lower lip.

"Are you excited now?" she said. The huskiness in her little-girl voice had shaded into hoarseness. Her eyes had narrowed until they were barely slitted. Her body had gotten more lax as she talked and her thighs had slid forward on the banquette seat until her skirt was merely ornamental. Her breath was short now, and audible. Her body seemed entirely inert, almost boneless, and yet the tension in her was manifest; physical slackness over tight-coiled emotion.

"No," I said.

There was silence. Jill Joyce stared at me through her barely open eyes.

"Whaaat?" she said.

I shrugged and flipped up my palms. I smiled engagingly.

More silence. More staring with her reptilian slits. She picked up her wineglass and drank most of it and lowered the glass and gazed at me over the rim of it. Then she threw the contents at me. She missed.

"Probably better than drinking it," I said.

"Sonovabitch," she said.

The flaccidity left her body. She rolled suddenly out of the banquette and stood in front of me and threw a punch with her clenched right fist. I blocked it with my left forearm.

"Oww," she said. "You bastard."

She swung at me with the other hand and I blocked that and she said "Ow" again and called me a bastard.

"Does this mean you're not going to call me dickie-bird anymore?" I said.

She was rubbing both wrists where I blocked her punches with my forearms, her shoulders bent, huddling over the sore arms.

"Limp dick, motherfucker," she said. Her voice sounded tight, as if her throat were closing. "Get the fuck out of here. You're fired, you prick."

"Fired," I said. "How can I be fired? I haven't been hired yet."

She lunged against me suddenly. Her face tilted up at me, her eyes closed all the way, her face very white except for two red spots that glowed feverishly on her cheekbones. Her mouth was open, her tongue protruded a little.

"You bastard," she gasped. "You better, you bastard. You better." Some tears squeezed out under the tightly closed lids. "You better," she said. Then she passed out on me. I caught her under the arms as she started to slide.

"Star quality," I said aloud.

I looked around the mobile home. Across the back was a big double bed with a pink puff on it, and half a dozen white pillows with lace ruffles. I turned and dragged Jill Joyce to the bed. Her legs were entirely limp. Her heels made little drag marks in the carpet. When I reached the bed, I got her over my hip and plumped her backside onto the bed and eased her down. She lay crossways, her feet still on the floor. Her skirt bunched up around her waist.

A voice said, "This would be more exciting in the pre-pantyhose era."

It was my voice and it sounded extraordinarily normal. I got hold of her ankles and half spun her around so her head was among the pillows and her feet were on the bed. Then I arranged her head so she wouldn't smother, and rearranged her skirt and put the mink coat over her.

The voice said, "What becomes a legend most."

It was me again. I sounded sane.

I stood back and looked down at her. Her cheeks were still wet with the faint tracing of tears. Her mouth was slightly open. She was snoring, not very loudly, but quite clearly. The only other noises in the mobile home were the faint hum of the refrigerator somewhere forward and a faint tingling sound which was probably from the heaters.

My voice seemed booming when it spoke again.

"You are a mess," my voice said thoughtfully, "you are a terrible mess."

I went out of the mobile home and closed the door carefully behind me.

4

I COLLECTED Susan from the wardrobe trailer, and we walked down across the Common toward Boylston Street. As the afternoon shortened it had gotten colder, and now in the late half-light of a winter afternoon the temperature was maybe ten above. The wind had died and it was still and brittle among the black trees. Around the Common the city lights had begun to show weakly, pale heatless flickers at the fringe of the hard silence. There was no one on the Common. Susan's shoulder touched mine as we walked. Her hands were jammed into the big pockets of her coat. Only a small white oval of her face showed inside the turned-up collar, under the fur hat, framed by the black hair. I had my hands in my jacket pockets. There were times for holding hands, and times for not. I had my watch cap pulled down over my ears too. It wasn't raffish but I knew Susan would let it pass.

"Cold, cold, cold, cold," Susan said.

"Cold," I said.

"Ah, the master of compression," Susan said. "How far is Biba?"

"Other side of Charles Street," I said.

Susan had been to Biba exactly as often as I had,

since she'd always gone with me. But she always asked distances like that as if she was just in from Boise.

At Charles Street the commuter traffic had started to develop and the exhaust of newly started engines plumed in the iron air. We crossed Charles and then Boylston and went past the Four Seasons Hotel and turned in under Biba's blue awning.

The bar was not crowded. The cold slowed everything down. Susan ordered a cup of tea with Courvoisier on the side. I had a brandy and soda. She had draped her coat open over the back of her chair and pulled off her gloves. Her face was bright with the cold. She kept the fur hat on and it seemed almost to blend with her thick black hair. Her chin rested on the heavy fold of a black turtleneck sweater. With our drinks we ordered some crab tacos and some empanadas. It was warm in the bar and I knew that upstairs the brick oven was baking bread. A hint of its warmth and smell drifted down, or it seemed to. I could feel the stiffness leave me as I drank maybe a third of the brandy and soda and felt the warmth under the cold soda ease through my system. I looked at Susan, at the width of her mouth, the fullness of her lower lip, the line of her cheekbone. I watched her dab a microscopic portion of salsa on one corner of a crabmeat taco and bite off an edge. It was a small taco, the kind you pop into your mouth all at once, if you're any kind of an eater at all. It would take Susan fifteen minutes to finish it. She chewed her tiny bite carefully, watching me look at her.

"So," she said, and her teeth flashed white and even as she smiled at me. "How do I stack up against Jill Joyce?"

I popped one of the empanadas into my mouth and chewed. I washed it down with more brandy and soda.

"I think I'd need to see you both naked before I can make a full judgment," I said.

Susan nodded thoughtfully.

"Well, I could arrange that at my end," she said.

"Nicely phrased," I said. "Jill has already made a similar offer."

Susan poured a splash of cognac into her tea, took a small sip, and put the teacup down. She watched a couple of guys in tweed overcoats and plaid scarves come in, rubbing their hands and hunching their shoulders from the cold. They crossed to the bar, put briefcases on the floor, and ordered Jack Daniel's on the rocks. Susan looked back at me. Her big dark eyes seemed bottomless.

"Hard to blame her," Susan said.

"Yes," I said, "of course it is. I think for her it was love at first sight."

"It happens to her a lot, I understand."

"You mean there's someone else?" I said.

Susan's smile widened. She sipped a little more tea, assessed its impact, added another small splash of cognac. "I think so," she said.

"Oh, well," I said. "There's always you."

"I adore it when you sweet-talk me," Susan said.

"Emphasis on the always," I said.

"Yes," Susan said. She finished the first crab taco. "So," she said, "she made a pass at you?"

"Almost an assault," I said.

"And you turned her down."

"I didn't get the chance to. She passed out."

"Tell me about it," Susan said. "Everything. Every detail."

I did. By the time I'd finished it was time for another brandy and soda. When it arrived I slid down a little in my chair and stretched out my legs in front of me and watched the amusement play on Susan's face. Outside in the darkness life barely moved in the sullen cold. Inside was food and drink and Susan and the whole evening ahead. Susan made the measuring gesture with her hands, mimicking Jill Joyce.

"This long?" she said. "Good heavens."

She looked at me, looked back at the measured distance between her hands, looked at me again, and slowly shook her head. I shrugged.

"I thought I could bluff it through," I said.

"You think that about everything," Susan said. "Are you going to take the job?"

I turned the glass around in little circles on the table in front of me, holding it lightly with both hands, watching it revolve.

"I don't know," I said.

"She's awfully difficult," Susan said. She had her

elbows on the table and she held her teacup in both hands, talking to me over the rim.

"Yeah," I said.

"Today was not unusual," Susan said.

"What about the four and a half pages they had to shoot this afternoon?" I said.

"Sandy will shoot around it," Susan said. "He's amazing."

"Why don't they just fire her?" I said. "Get someone who's sober all day?"

"TVQ," Susan said and smiled like she does when she's able to kid me and herself at the same time.

The maître d' came over and told us our table was ready for dinner.

"Whenever you're ready, sir. No hurry."

He went back to his post near the door.

"TVQ?" I said sadly.

"Television Quotient. It's a way of rating star appeal," she said.

"Of course," I said.

"Jill Joyce has the highest TVQ of anyone now on television," Susan said.

"And to think she wanted to jump on my bones," I said. "Makes you feel sort of humble, doesn't it?"

"And a TVQ like that translates into ratings which translate into renewal which translates eventually into a big syndication deal which translates . . ."

"Into money," I said.

"Bingo," Susan said. "Mucho dinero, sweetheart."

"Have you gone, just a twidge, ah, Hollywood?" I said.

"I'll say. Film is my life." Susan's eyes crinkled and her smile was brighter than Jill Joyce's TVQ.

"And it doesn't cut into your work?"

"My patients? No. Nothing cuts into that."

"Nothing? I remember a Monday morning three months ago . . ."

"Except you," Susan said. "Occasionally, and, if it's the Monday morning I'm thinking about, I feel that you overpowered me. That doesn't count."

"Then how come I was on the bottom?"

"Just never mind," Susan said. "It's time to go up for dinner."

We went up and sat and looked at the menus. The room looked out over the Public Garden which was lit with concealed spots and stiller than death in the brute cold evening.

"Actually," Susan said as she scanned the menu, "my formal duties don't require me to be on the set. I read scripts and make suggestions. That's really the extent of my technical advice. The rest of the time I come around and watch because it fascinates me."

I nodded, contemplating the herbed chicken with mashed potatoes.

"It doesn't fascinate you?" Susan said.

"Fascinated me for about ten minutes," I said. "But I gather they do this for more than ten minutes."

"Twelve hours a day," Susan said. "Six days a week. More if they're behind."

"And a show starring Jill Joyce often gets behind," I said.

"Sandy and most of the directors have worked with her before," Susan said. "They try to arrange to shoot most of her scenes before lunch. Close-ups and stuff. Long scenes they can use a double, or they can loop her dialogue afterwards."

"Loop her dialogue," I said.

"Aren't I awful?" Susan said. She smiled happily about it. "I'm totally stagestruck. I talk the jargon. I'm not sure I can be saved."

"In fact, one of the eighty-two things, by actual count, that I like about you is the totality of your enthusiasms," I said.

"What are the other eighty-one?" Susan said.

"I think I mentioned them to you that Monday morning."

"Actually, I think you concentrated rather heavily that day on maybe one or two," she said.

The waitress came, we ordered, the waitress went away. Susan leaned toward me a little, her chin resting on her folded hands. The play was gone from her eyes.

"Actually, I hope you will help her," she said.

"Jill Joyce?"

"Yes. I don't know if someone's bothering her or not; but she is so lost."

"I'm supposed to be the detective," I said. "You're supposed to be the shrink."

"I can't help her," Susan said. "She won't come near me. She doesn't have anyone. Sandy tries to take care of her, but he's got to make the pictures. She has no one who's simply looking out for her. Not because of her TVQ, or the syndication deal we can get five years down the road. Not because she's Jill Joyce."

"Think anyone's ever done that?" I said.

"No," Susan said.

I looked out at the Public Garden, at the leafless willows through whose spidery branches the back lighting showed.

"And you think I should," I said.

"Yes."

"Even at the risk of my, ah . . ." I held my hands out in the two-foot measuring motion.

Susan smiled at me as sweetly as a convent acolyte.

"You have little to lose," she said.

5

I SAT in the production office on Soldiers Field Road and talked with Sandy Salzman. Without his tasseled ski cap he was balding.

"Do you want me to protect Miss Joyce," I said, "or do you want me to find out who's harassing her?"

"Or *if*," Salzman said. Through the picture window in his office you could look across Soldiers Field Road at the Charles River, and across the Charles to Cambridge on the other side. The river was frozen now and snow covered. There were cross-country ski tracks on it, and trampled paths where kids and dogs had cut across. It was a steady-moving river, and it took a deep chill to freeze it enough to walk on. Every year there was a thaw and someone went through.

"Or *if*," I said. "But someone needs to decide. I can't do both at the same time."

"What's Jill say?"

"Jill says she's looking for one this long." I made the measuring motion for him.

"Yeah, Jill says stuff like that," Salzman said. "What'd you say?"

"I told her she was in luck."

Salzman laughed.

"Then she had another glass of wine and fainted at me."

Salzman nodded. "She does that too," he said.

"Makes a swell date," I said.

Salzman spread his hands and shrugged. "Jill's a television star," he said. "She's been one for twenty years in a medium where a lot of people are reading weather in Topeka six months after their first show is canceled. You got Jill Joyce on a project and you've got a thirteen-week on-air commitment, and all three networks fighting to make it."

"That explains why she gets loaded every lunch and swoons on strangers?" I said.

"No, it explains why she gets away with it."

"So which is it? Protect her or investigate the incidents, whatever the hell they are, no one seems too clear on that."

"I know," Salzman said. "The truth is, nobody pays a hell of a lot of attention to Jill beyond keeping her in shape to go on. Line producer earns his money on one of her shows."

"So you don't know what you want me to do," I said. "But you haven't got time to deal with her."

Salzman tapped the sharpened end of a prone pencil on his desk, causing it to flip up and somersault in the air.

"Exactly," he said and jabbed his forefinger toward me while he said it.

There were pictures all around the office, most of

Salzman; a couple with actors, the rest with dead pheasant and elk and trout.

"Okay," I said. "I'll talk to Jill and I'll decide what I should do. If I decide I need to do both, I'll hire someone to watch Jill while I investigate."

"You have someone in mind?" Salzman said. "Jill is very tough about people."

I grinned. "Yeah," I said. "I got a guy in mind."

It made me happy, thinking of Hawk with Jill Joyce.

Salzman frowned a little, but he let it pass. He was affable in the Hollywood way, and permanently pleasant, but behind it there was a pretty good mind working. And most of the time it was working on getting his show made on time, on budget. He knew when to go with the flow, and if I'd take the matter of Jill Joyce's harassment off his back he'd agree to hiring Geraldo Rivera as a bodyguard if I said so. He knew that. I knew that. And he knew that I knew that.

"We got you through the police commissioner," Salzman said. "Commissioner himself said you were good."

"Man loves me," I said.

"Actually," Salzman said, "he remarked that he didn't like you a bit, but you were the best at what you did."

"Same thing," I said. "Where's the lovely Miss Joyce?"

"We're shooting here today. Too cold out for Jill."

Salzman got up.

"I'll take you down. Ever seen film being made?"

"Yeah," I said.

"Exciting?"

"Like watching ice melt," I said.

"I can see you're a fan," Salzman said.

We went out through the outer office where two young women hunched over typewriters. There was a fax machine on the window sill, and six file cabinets, and on the wall a big, and detailed, map of Boston.

"I'll be on the set," Salzman said to one of the young women. She nodded without looking up.

"Remember you've got the teamster guys at eleven forty-five," she said.

"Page me when they arrive," Salzman said. We went down the corridor past glassed-in office space where people labored over computers and drawing boards and typewriters. We went down the stairs and through the lobby, with a huge promotional poster of Jill Joyce on the wall, and a receptionist at her desk, and down another corridor, past the wardrobe office and the property room and the carpenter shop to a sound stage. On the thick door to the sound stage was a big sign that said DO NOT ENTER WHEN RED LIGHT IS ON. Above the door was a red light. It was on. Salzman opened the door quietly and we went in. We were on the back side of some walls that had been assembled from plywood and two-by-fours. On the other side of those walls the space was brightly lit. I followed Salzman around the cluster of ragged crew members loitering off camera, waiting to do what they were employed to do.

The set was of an office, or two walls of an office, in which a psychiatrist, Dr. Shannon Cassidy, was confronting an obviously demented man who was armed with a Browning automatic and was pointing it at her the way everybody points guns on television, with two hands, straight out, at shoulder level. Shannon was played by the delectable Jill Joyce, clear-eyed, kind, intuitive yet passionate, in a crisply tailored suit. In her bearing and in every word she spoke there was the kind of wise and sexy innocence that had guaranteed thirteen-week on-air pickups for twenty years. The demented man was a guest star whom I'd never heard of.

"You make any sudden moves, Doc," the demented man was saying, "and you're gonna be real sorry."

Dr. Cassidy's smile was caring and brave.

"Don't you realize, Kenneth, that you're the victim?" Doc Cassidy said. "I can't let you hurt yourself this way . . . someone does care."

She slowly extended her hand.

"I care."

She held her hand out toward the guy, whose face ran the gamut of emotions from A to B. His face contorted, the gun shook.

"You're not alone if someone cares," Doc Cassidy said softly.

The demented guy suddenly lunged forward and put the gun into her hand. The director said "Cut."

And the demented guy straightened up and took his hands from his face and stopped being demented.

"Who writes this stuff?" he said.

A grayish woman with ample hips came around the desk where Jill Joyce was sitting. She wore a hand mirror on a ribbon around her waist and she held it in front of Jill while she made small dabbing motions at Jill's hair with a little bristly brush. A make-up woman also appeared and dusted Jill's face with a small, soft brush, the kind you might use to baste a spare rib. A young production assistant in jeans and a man's flannel shirt handed Jill a lit cigarette and Jill dragged on it intently while make-up and hair hovered over her.

"Places," the director said. Without his earflaps he was a thin-faced man with short reddish hair.

An assistant director said, "Quiet, everybody." Then he said, "Rolling for picture."

The director said "Action."

And they did the scene again. The sound man with his earphones, hovering over the sound console, said "Cut" after the demented guest star said his first line.

"We're picking up a whir, Rich."

Somebody went around the corner of the set and said something I couldn't hear and came back.

"Okay?" he said.

The director looked at the sound man.

"Okay," the sound man said.

And the scene rolled again, and then again.

"First one was the cover shot," Salzman whispered between takes. "Others are for close-ups, so when they get it back in L.A. in the editing room, Milo and the film editor can cross-cut, you know?"

"Un huh," I said.

"What do you think?" Salzman said.

"I think you're hiring me for the wrong job," I said. "I think you should hire me to go beat up the writers."

Salzman shrugged. "Hard cranking out a script a week," he said.

"Obviously," I said.

6

"WELL, well," Jill Joyce said as she came off the set. "The cutie-pie cop with the big muscles."

"I didn't think you'd noticed," I said.

"You here to take care of me?" she said. Her on-camera make-up was a little heavy, but standing there in front of me she was fresh-faced and beautiful. Her cheeks dimpled as she spoke. Her skin was clear and smooth, her eyes sparkled with life and a hint of innocent sexuality. She looked like orange juice and fresh laundry, the perfect date for the Williams-Amherst game, in a plaid skirt, picnicking beforehand on a blanket. Her lips would taste like apples. Her hair would smell like honey. Fresh-scrubbed, spunky, compliant, brave, beautiful, decent, cute. With a TVQ that made your breath come short.

"I'm here to discuss it," I said.

"Your place or mine?" Jill said and dimpled at me.

"Your place," I said, "but remember, I'm armed."

Jill giggled deep in her throat.

"I hope so," she said. She looked at the director. "Half an hour, Rich?"

"Sure, Jilly," the director said. "No more, though, I'm trying to bring this thing in under, for once."

"Maybe you could make your mind up where to put the fucking camera, Rich," Jill said. She spoke without heat, almost absently, as she walked away.

I followed her, watching her hips sway as she walked. Her back was perfectly straight. Her hair was glossy and thick. The skirt fit smoothly over her elegant backside. We went out a side door into the cold, walked twenty feet to Jill's mobile home and went in. Jill was all business today. She sat in the driver's seat sideways, crossed her legs, rested her left arm on the steering wheel.

"Okay, cutie," she said. "Talk."

I didn't answer. I was looking down the length of the mobile home toward the bed. Above the bed, suspended from a ceiling fixture, was a plastic doll, dressed in a gold lamé evening gown, hanging with a miniature slipknot around her neck. Jill saw me looking and shifted her glance, and saw the swaying doll.

"What's that?" she said.

I walked down the length of the mobile home and looked more closely at the doll without touching it. I could hear Jill's footsteps behind me. The doll gazed at me from a face that looked a little like Jill Joyce, its happy smile entirely incongruous above the hangman's knot around its throat. The knot caused the doll to cant at an angle. I could feel Jill press against me. Her hand was on my arm just above the elbow. She squeezed.

"What is that?" she said.

"Just a doll," I said. "You recognize it?"

She stayed behind me but moved her head around for a closer look, her cheek pressed against my upper arm. She looked for a moment.

"Jesus God," she said.

"Yeah?" I said.

"It's me," she said. "It's me."

She slid around over my arm and pressed herself against me, both arms around me, her head against my chest.

"It's a doll of me," she said, "as Tiffany Scott."

Even I had heard of Tiffany Scott, the spunky, lovable girl reporter, caught up in a series of hair-raising adventures, week after week, for six years on ABC. It was the series that had made her the preeminent television star in the country. Her body was tighter against me than my gunbelt and she seemed to insinuate herself at very precarious spots.

"Got any theories?" I said.

"He did it," she said. Her voice was hoarse, throaty with fear. "It's . . ." She squeezed tighter against me. I would not have thought that possible, but she did it. "It's a warning." Her breath was short, and audible.

"Who's he?" I said. Spenser, master detective, asker of the penetrating questions.

"I don't know," she said.

"Then how do you know it's him?" I said. "Or is it he?"

"He's done things like this before."

"He has," I said. "But we don't know who he is."

I was losing control of my pronouns. "Or whom?" I said.

She turned her face in against me.

"It's not funny," she said.

I reached up with my free hand, the one she wasn't clinging to, and took the doll down.

"His name isn't Ken, is it?"

"I told you," she said. "I don't know who he is. I just know he's after me."

I got my arm free of her clutch and turned her around and steered her back to the front of the mobile home.

"I'll need to talk to your driver," I said.

"Paulie," she said.

"Paulie what?"

"I don't know. I just call him Paulie. You got a cigarette?"

"I don't smoke," I said.

"Well, hand me some from the table there," she said.

I gave her the cigarettes and she took one out and put it into her mouth and looked at me expectantly. There were matches on the dashboard in front of the driver's seat. I stood, stepped past her, took a book of matches and lit her cigarette, then I tucked the matches inside the cellophane wrapper on the cigarette pack and put them in her lap.

"Who would know Paulie's full name?" I said.

"I don't know, for God's sake, ask Sandy. I don't

keep track of every sweat hog that works on this picture."

"The bigger they are, the nicer they are."

She seemed recovered from her panic.

"You do coke?" she said.

I shook my head.

"Well, I do," she said. "You got a problem with that?"

I shook my head again. She went to the breakfast nook, got the stuff out of a cabinet and did two lines off the tabletop.

"I got to work this afternoon," she said. "You try getting up every time the light goes on. You try sparkling eight hours a day, sometimes ten or fifteen."

"For me, it's easy," I said, and gave her a sparkling smile.

She paid me no attention. She was bobbing her head slightly and tapping her fingers on the tabletop.

"You going to do something about this?" she said.

I looked at her, jeeped from the coke, waiting to go out and pretend to be wonderful; evasive and self-deluded and kind of stupid, and startlingly beautiful. For all I knew she'd hung the doll herself. For all I knew "he" didn't exist.

"Are you?" she said. She was impatient now, tapping her foot, her eyes very bright. "I've got to go to work. I need to know."

Still I stared at her. She was trouble, alcoholic, drug addicted, nymphomaniac, egocentric, spoiled brat trouble. She leaned a little toward me, her eyes the size of dahlias. She moistened her lower lip with the tip of her tongue.

"Are you?" she said. "Please?"

"Yeah," I said. "I'm going to do something about this."

She nodded her head too many times and then headed out toward the sound stage. I was reminded of a child, off to kindergarten, frightened, sad, trying to be grown up; marching off like a little soldier, with two lines of coke up her nose.

7

PAULIE spent most of his time downstairs in the production office drinking coffee with the other drivers. Someone beeped him when Miss Joyce was ready. Anyone could have wandered in there and hung the doll.

The transportation captain, a big gray-haired guy named Mickey Boylan, sat in while I talked with Paulie.

"You need any help on this, you let me know," he said when Paulie had told me all he knew. And maybe a little more. "This show is good for us, gotta lot of people driving."

Boylan was a business agent with the union.

"I'll take anything I can get," I said.

"You think there's somebody really after her?" Boylan said.

"I guess so," I said. "Otherwise what am I doing here?"

Boylan grinned. "This sow's got a lot of tits," he said. "Could feed one more easy enough."

I gave Boylan my card.

"I hate to spin my wheels," I said. "Even for money."

"No other reason to do it," Boylan said as I left.

I wandered back down to the sound stage and leaned against the wall out of the way and waited for Jill Joyce. Watching a television show being filmed was like watching dandruff form. It was a long, slow process and when you were through, what did you have? Maybe Boylan was right. Maybe this was just a boondoggle and I was getting paid to make Jill Joyce feel good. She had yet to tell me a goddamned thing about herself. The hanging doll was easy to fake and came at the right time. I didn't even know what other harassment there had been. So why didn't I take a walk? The money was good, but there's always money. Why didn't I walk right now instead of standing around listening to some of the worst dialogue ever uttered, over and over again? I had my leather jacket hanging on a light tripod. Now and then someone would glance my way and do a short double-take at the gun under my left arm. The rest of the time things were much calmer. My head itched. The watch cap made my hair sweaty, but if I took it off, the way it matted my hair down made me look like an oversized rock musician.

On set, out of sight, but sadly not out of hearing, Jill Joyce was selling the closing lines of her scene for the fifth time.

"Where there's love," she said, "there's a chance."

I knew why I was waiting for her. It was what Susan had said at dinner. *She doesn't have anyone to look out for her.* There was something so small and alone in her, so unconnected and frightened, that I couldn't walk away from her. If she was staging these harassments she needed help. If she wasn't staging them she needed help. I was better equipped to give one kind of help than I was the other. And equipped or not, whatever she needed, I was the only one willing.

At 4:25 the director said, "That's it, thanks, Jilly. See you tomorrow." And without answering, Jill Joyce walked around the set partition and stopped in front of me.

"You'll drive me home," she said.

"Yes," I said.

The people who'd been lounging around glancing at my gun were now busy dismantling the set wall in front of us. They swung it out to open up the set and two people moved the camera dolly around into the space where I was standing.

"Excuse me," someone said, "coming through."

"We'll get my coat in wardrobe," Jill said.

"Sure."

I followed her off the sound stage and down the corridor past the carpenter shop to the wardrobe office. Jill went in and came out in a moment wearing a silver-tipped mink.

"Kathleen," she spoke back through the open door, "did Ernie get me that white sable we talked about?"

A woman's voice from the wardrobe office said, "Got it right here, Jilly."

"Excellent," Jill said. "I'll come in tomorrow for a fitting."

"Give us a little notice if you can," the woman's voice said.

Jill didn't answer, nor did she appear to have heard the request for notice. We went on out through the production office and into the front parking lot where I had my car.

"You need to tell anybody, drivers, anyone like that?" I said.

Jill made a dismissive motion with her hand.

"Which car is yours?" she said.

"The glorious black Cherokee," I said. "Ideal for all-weather surveillance."

"Well, it's better than I expected," she said.

I held the door, she got in, ran a hand over the leather upholstery, and nodded approvingly.

"The Charles Hotel?" I said.

"In Cambridge. You know where it is?"

I did my Bogart impression with the flattened upper lip. "I know where everything is, sweetheart."

She got out a cigarette, pressed in my lighter and waited for it to pop. When it did she put it against the cigarette and the pleasing smell of tobacco lit with a car lighter filled the front seat. She put the lighter back and leaned her hand against the back of the seat with the cigarette glowing in her mouth and closed her eyes. Her face was very white and still, nestled in the big collar of her fur coat. Without raising her hand to the cigarette, she took a big drag and let the smoke out slowly from the corners of her mouth. The early winter evening had settled around us, and the automobile headlights on Soldiers Field

Road had a pale cold look to them. I let the motor idle while I looked at her, her hands plunged deep into the pockets of her mink, her body tucked well inside it, a little shivery from the cold as we waited for the heater. In the faint light she looked about twelve, except for the glowing cigarette, a tired child, not yet pubescent, the apple unbitten on the tree, the serpent yet to tempt her.

"I need a drink," she said.

I didn't say anything. Across the river lights were popping on as people came home from work. The mercury lamp street lights on our side of the river had the weak orange look they get before it's fully dark and they turn blue-white. Wind whipped a small dervish of powdery snow off the frozen river and spun it west where the river turned toward Watertown.

"I said I need a drink." Jill spoke around a slow drift of smoke.

"Yes, you did," I said.

"Well for Christ's sake, do something about it."

"Maybe I could siphon off a little gasoline?"

"Don't be cute with me, stupid. Just get this thing in gear and get us to the hotel."

"I saw Gene Tierney do that once," I said. "Smoked a cigarette just like that. Head back, eyes closed. And Sterling Hayden was her boyfriend . . ."

"Will you drive this fucking car?" she said.

I did.

8

THE doorman at the Charles Hotel was a young guy with a go-to-hell Irish face made red by the cold. He wore a fur-collared greatcoat and the kind of hat Russian ministers wear. He said he'd hold my car for me.

"No problem," he said, and started the revolving door turning for Jill Joyce as she preceded me into the lobby.

"Come up for a drink," she said.

"Last time I came to your place for a drink you attempted to molest me," I said.

She turned with her mink coat open and her hands on her hips. She tossed her head back a little and her pelvis forward a little.

"You scared?" she said.

"Yuh," I said.

She shook her head in disgust. "Like most men," she said, "never had a real woman."

I let that pass. Discussing it in the lobby of the Charles Hotel didn't seem like a way to bring clarity to the argument.

"Buy me a drink in the Quiet Bar," she said. "Then if I frighten you, you can yell for the house dick."

"Okay," I said, "but you've got to promise to talk with me."

We started up the wide staircase to the second level of the Charles.

"Talk to you?" She stopped one step ahead of me and turned and looked back.

"With," I said.

She shook her head in open amazement, and continued up the stairs, talking over her shoulder.

"What are you?" she asked. "Queer? You some kinda faggot?"

"You're going to have to talk with me," I said, "about yourself, your past, your fans, your lovers."

"You get your rocks off talking?" she said. Her voice was loud. "You are a fucking queer."

I took a quick two steps and caught her from behind and lifted her, holding her by her upper arms, up the last stair and steered her around the stairwell into an alcove near and to the left of the entrance to the bar. Her feet were still clear of the ground. She started to twist loose, but with her feet in the air she didn't have much purchase.

"I'm tired of you," I said. "I was tired of you halfway through lunch the first time I met you. But you need some help, and there doesn't seem to be anyone else but me. So I'm hanging in there, and I haven't hit you yet. But I will soon if it keeps going the way it's going."

I gave her a little shake.

"You understand that?" I said.

Her breath was coming in little gasps.

I shook her again.

"You understand?"

Still making her gasping sound, she nodded her head.

"Now," I said, "I'm going to ask you about things, and you're going to answer me and we're not going to play all this seductive teenager grab-ass that we've been playing. Right?"

She nodded again.

I set her down and let go of her upper arms. She leaned forward against the wall for a moment, and then turned slowly, leaning on the wall as she did, and rubbed her upper arms with her hands. Her breathing was still a series of half-stifled gasps and two bright streaks of crimson color smudged along her cheekbones.

"Limp . . . dick . . . mother . . . fucker," she gasped, and then fell forward and began to sob against my chest. The sobbing wasn't loud but it was wracking. Her whole body shook with it. Her arms hung straight down and still against her sides. I put my arms around her and patted her back gently while she cried. Two couples got off the elevator and came around the corner and studiously didn't look at us. The men wore dark suits and red ties. The women wore frilly dresses with padded shoulders. Both men and women had too much hair. In from the suburbs. I had on a leather jacket and jeans and my Adidas Countries—white leather with the green stripes. An oldie but goodie. One of the women glanced back as they headed into the bar. Probably admiring the rakish cant to my watch cap.

Jill stopped sobbing after a while. But she kept her face pressed against my chest.

"Ready for that drink?" I said.

"I can't go in there," she said. Her voice was muffled. "I look awful."

"You could look twice as bad," I said, "and still look wonderful."

She leaned away from me and raised her face. It was red and her eyes were puffy and some of her make-up was tear-washed. I revised my opinion, but kept it to myself.

"You mean it?" she said.

"Absolutely," I said.

She fumbled some Kleenex out of her purse and dabbed at her eyes.

"Show must go on," I said.

"Give me five minutes," she said, "in the ladies' room."

"Okay."

We walked to the ladies' room.

"I'll be right outside the door. You need me, you holler."

"And you'll come in and catch all the Cambridge ladies making peepee?"

"Cambridge ladies don't do that," I said.

She smiled at me softly, with her head down, moving only her eyes to look up at me. It was a wan smile, I think. Then she went into the ladies' room and I leaned on the wall outside. For more than five minutes. One of the suburban ladies who'd admired my watch cap admired it again as she went past me into the ladies' room, and admired it at even greater length when she came out a few minutes later.

"This a technique for picking up girls?" she said.

"Have you fallen for me because of my watch cap?" I said.

"No," she said and walked off.

It was maybe fifteen minutes and I was beginning to wonder when I heard Jill Joyce scream, "Spenser!"

I slammed through the ladies' room door with my gun out, did a little deke around a partition, and there I was. A startled woman in a green paisley dress was just emerging from a stall. She froze when she saw the gun and then ducked back into the stall. At the far end of the ladies' room in front of the handicapped stall Jill Joyce stood with her mouth a little open, her eyes glittering, her arms folded across her breast, right hand holding left elbow. There was no one else in there. The other stall doors were ajar.

"Testing?" I said.

She laughed. It wasn't a good laugh; it was off-key and it wobbled up and down the scale, teetering on hysteria. I slid my gun back under my arm out of sight, inside my jacket.

"I wondered if you'd really burst into a ladies' lounge."

"You through in here?" I said.

She did her fluty laugh again.

"For now," she said.

I jerked my head toward the door and started out. She followed me. We walked across the lobby and into the cocktail lounge. There was a bar with stools along the left wall. In the rest of the room were couches and easy chairs grouped around low cocktail tables. We got a grouping for two in a corner near the big windows that opened out onto the courtyard. In the summer there were umbrellas out there and tables and jazz concerts on Wednesday nights. Now there was a huge Christmas tree and the residue of vigorously removed snow. People walking from the shops to the hotel hunched stiffly against the cold.

The waitress came by. Jill ordered a double vodka martini. I had a beer. When she came back with the drinks she brought two dishes of smoked almonds. I nodded toward the bartender. He nodded back and gave me a thumbs-up gesture.

"Why two?" Jill said.

"Bartender knows me," I said and took a handful of nuts. Jill took a long pull on her martini. She looked at my glass.

"Beer?" she said.

"Very good," I said.

"You don't have to be a wise guy," she said. Her eyes were only a touch red now, and her make-up was all back in place. Her eyes were the color of cornflowers.

"I know," I said. "I do it voluntarily."

She drank another third of her martini and with only a third left her eyes already began to flick about looking for the waitress.

"Aside from the doll hanging," I said, "what instances have there been of harassment?"

She drank the rest of her martini, and again her eyes flicked around the room. I looked over at the bartender, who saw me and nodded. Jill shook a cigarette from the pack she'd placed on the table and put it in her mouth and leaned toward me. There were matches in the ashtray. I lit her cigarette, blew out the match and put it in the ashtray. I put the book of matches beside her cigarettes.

"What instances of harassment have there been?" I said. When interrogating a suspect, cleverly rephrasing the question is often effective.

"I think this is harassment," Jill said, her eyes searching for the waitress. "We have a nice evening together and you just want to talk about icky business."

"Icky business is my profession," I said. "Tell me about the harassment."

The waitress arrived with another double martini.

Jill said, "Ah."

The waitress looked at my beer, saw that it was nearly untouched, and went away. Jill dipped right in. I waited. Jill looked at me with her lovely innocent cornflower-blue eyes. I crossed my legs and tossed my foot a little to pass the time.

"Phone calls," Jill said. "Mostly phone calls."

"From a man?"

"Yes." There was surprise in Jill's voice, as if only men would ever call her.

"Where'd the calls come?"

"You mean where did I get them?"

"Un huh."

"On the phone in my mobile home. Here, at the hotel."

"There's been enough press about this show so that anyone would know you were staying here. How about the mobile home. How would he get that number?"

"*I* don't know. How, for Christ's sake, would *I* know?"

"Is it listed?"

She shook her head in disgust and flapped her hands in front of her, the cigarette smoking in her right one.

"Spenser, I don't know about stuff like that. I don't know if it's listed or not. Some gopher takes care of that. Ask Sandy, or the UPM."

"UPM?"

"Unit production manager, for God's sake. Why didn't they get somebody who at least knows something about the business."

"What's the name of the unit production manager?"

"Bob," Jill said. She was well into the second double martini.

"Bob what?" I said.

Jill flapped her hands again and shook her head.

"You think I memorize lists of names? I have to memorize sixty pages of dialogue every week. I don't have time to get chummy with every member of the office staff."

"Uneasy lies the head that wears a crown," I said.

"Where's that from?" Jill said.

"Some play," I said. "What did this caller say when he called?"

"Different stuff. Sex stuff, mostly."

"Like what?" I said.

"That a turn-on for you?" Jill said. "Having me talk about it?"

"Sure is," I said. "This whole conversation is more exciting than dinner with Jesse Helms."

Jill frowned beautifully, a lovely vertical frown line appearing briefly between her eyebrows and smoothing out at once.

"Whoever he is," she said. "Mostly this guy told me what he'd like to do to me when he got me alone."

"Abusive?" I said.

She was sipping her martini now; apparently the edge of need had softened.

"Actually," she said, "no. It wasn't, it was more, you know, ah, romantic."

"Romantic?"

"Yeah, lovey-dovey. Except he used all the dirty words. But he used them, like, romantically."

I nodded.

"And you don't, I suppose, have even a guess as to who he might be?" I said.

"If I did, you think I wouldn't have already told you? What kind of dumb jerk question is that?"

"The kind if you don't ask, you feel like a fool when it comes out that you should have asked."

"No, I don't know the guy. I don't recognize his voice. I don't have any idea who he is."

"Any letters?"

She shook her head. The martini was gone. She gestured at the waitress.

"No."

"Get any recordings of his calls?"

"No."

"Not on any answering machines, or anything?"

"I don't have answering machines," Jill said. The waitress brought her a third martini. I didn't have too much longer before talking with her would be useless.

Jill giggled. "I don't know how they work."

"You get any fan letters that seem odd?" I said.

"They're all odd," Jill said. "I mean, for crissake, fan letters."

"Any unusually odd?"

"I don't know. I don't read them. Ask Sandy."

"Sandy reads them?"

"Sandy, or some girl in the office. I don't have time for it. Somebody reads them and writes up a little cover, saying how they sound. You know? If there's a trend."

"Do you read that?" I said.

"No, they send it to my agent."

"Whose name is?"

"My agent?"

"Un huh."

"Why do you want my agent's name?"

"So I can talk with him," I said. "See, I'm a detective. That means I make an attempt to detect what's going on, by asking questions. By looking for, ah, clues. Stuff like that."

"You're making fun of me," Jill said.

"One would have to have a heart of stone . . ." I said.

"I get you in bed, I'd show you something," Jill said. She got another cigarette and leaned toward me while I lit it, her eyes fixed on me in a look that, I think, was supposed to make my blood race.

"What's your agent's name?" I said.

She leaned back and blew smoke out at me in disgust.

"Ken Craig," she said.

"He in L.A.?"

"Yes."

"How about relationships? Any that have ended lately?"

"Relationships?"

"Yeah. Marriages, lovers, business arrangements, anybody that you've cut loose that might be mad at you?"

Jill was holding the martini glass in both hands and resting it against her lower lip. She gazed at me over it, her eyes closed a little so that she had a smoky look.

"There are things a girl doesn't talk about to a man," she said.

"Aren't you the same woman who expressed an interest in something this long?" I said. I made the measuring gesture with my hands.

Her eyes widened and seemed to get brighter. The rim of her glass was still pressed against her lower lip; the tip of her tongue appeared above it and darted laterally, back and forth.

"Maybe I did," she said.

"And now there's things a girl doesn't discuss with a man?" I said.

She tilted the martini glass up suddenly and drank the rest of it in a long swallow. She put the glass down with a thump and stood up.

"I'm going to bed," she said.

The brightness left her eyes and they seemed unfocused now.

"I'm not saying another word to you. I'm going to bed."

"My loss," I said. She walked toward the elevator without another sound. I glanced at the bartender. He spread his hands, palms down in a don't-worry-about-it gesture. I left my beer half drunk and followed her out.

9

At 6:10 the winter morning was as bright as a hooker's promise and warmer than her heart. The temperature was already in the thirties and by noon the plowed streets would be dark and glistening with snow melt. I was in the lobby of the Charles Hotel, fresh showered, clean shaven, armed to the teeth, and dressed to the nines: sneakers, jeans, a black polo shirt, and a leather jacket. The collar of the polo shirt was turned up inside the collar of the jacket. I took off my Ray-Bans to see if I could catch another glimpse of myself in some lobby glass, but there wasn't any. I'd have to live on memories till we got to a mirror. I could go outside and look at myself in the smoked glass windows of the Lincoln Town Car parked out there, but the slight curve of the window enlarged things, and when you're a fifty regular you don't want enlargement.

At the far end of the lobby a solitary desk clerk shuffled paper behind the counter. A tall guy with rimless glasses was admiring the huge floral display in the middle of the lobby. Faintly, I could smell coffee, as, in the recesses of the building, the kitchen began to crank up for breakfast. Past the floral display, to the left of the wide staircase, an elevator door opened and Jill Joyce came out, along with a bulky black man in a blue blazer. The black man carried a walkie-talkie. He nodded when he saw me and moved away, and she was mine for the day.

Jill was wearing jeans which appeared to have been applied with a spray gun, high emerald boots with three-inch heels, a white blouse unbuttoned to exactly the right depth of cleavage. She had her black mink coat thrown over her shoulders. Until you got very close she looked as if she weren't wearing any make-up. Close up I could see that she was, and that it was so artfully applied that it gave the illusion of fresh-faced innocence, with a touch of lip gloss. She was carrying an alligator bag that was either a large purse or the carrying case for a small tuba. She handed it to me.

"Good morning, cute buns," I said.

"I was hoping you'd notice."

We went out through the revolving door. The tall guy with the rimless glasses went out through the swinging doors to the left of the revolving door and when we reached the sidewalk he said, "Miss Joyce."

Jill shook her head.

"Not now," she said. "I've got a six-fifteen call."

He moved very smoothly for a geek, and he was in her path and saying, "Miss Joyce, Mr. Rojack wishes to speak with you."

I moved between Jill and the tall guy. "What is your wish?" I said to Jill.

"I want to go to work," she said.

"Miss Joyce prefers to go to work," I said to the tall guy.

The tall guy's voice flattened out like a piece of hammered tin.

"Buzz off," he said.

"Buzz off?" I said. "Buzz? Off? Which one are you? Archie? Or Jughead?"

The tall guy's face reddened, but not enough. He was very pale with short white-blond hair and a big Adam's apple. He put one hand, his left, gently on my chest.

"Just back off, cowboy," he said. "You don't know what you're getting into."

I didn't like him putting his hand on me, but defending my honor was not the first order of business here.

"Let's go," I said to Jill.

I moved to the left of the tall guy, keeping Jill behind me. My car was parked on the walkway, back of the limo with the tinted windows. As we moved, one of the windows slid silently down and a guy with a fine profile looked out.

"Randall," the guy with the fine profile said, "get rid of him."

The tall guy smiled. The hand on my chest slid over and gripped my leather jacket. He started to turn his left hip in toward me when I kneed him in the groin. He grunted and started to sag. I turned my left shoulder in on myself and brought up a left uppercut that straightened him against, then bounced him off the car. His head banged against the edge of the car roof and he slid down the door and sat with his legs sprawled in front of him on the cold brick of the hotel turnaround.

Behind me Jill said, "Jesus," softly.

I bent and looked into the car at the man with the profile. He wasn't showing it to me. He was showing me full face, and there was a gun in his hand.

"Wow," I said. "A Sig Sauer, just like the cops are getting."

Profile said to me, "What the hell is your name?"

"Zorro," I said. "I forgot my cape."

"Never seen anyone deal with Randall quite like that."

"Randall's too confident," I said. "Makes him careless."

"Perhaps this will have been good for him."

"I surely hope so," I said.

Profile looked past me at Jill Joyce.

"I've been trying to reach you, Jill," he said.

She didn't look at him.

"You've not returned my calls."

"Come on," Jill said to me. "We're late already."

I straightened.

"I won't be put off, Jill," the Profile said.

Jill started to walk away. I straightened from the window.

"See you around," I said.

"Yes, you will," the Profile said.

"Tell Randall," I said, "that hip throw went out about the same time *buzz off* did."

"Perhaps he knows that now," the Profile said. "I'm sure you'll see him again too."

I followed Jill and got there in time to hold the door for her. As I pulled out around the Town Car, I saw the Profile getting out and walking around toward where Randall sat on the cold bricks.

We drove out past the Kennedy School and right onto JFK Street and headed out across the Larz Anderson Bridge.

"What was that in the car?" I said. "Darryl F. Zanuck?"

"I have no idea," she said.

"About many things, I think that's true," I said. "About the guy in the car—I don't believe you."

The Anderson Bridge looks like a bridge that would connect Cambridge to Boston. It is short. The river here was maybe a hundred yards wide. The bridge arched the way bridges do over the Seine, and was made of brick, or seemed to be, having enough brick dressing to fool your eye. To the right the river was broad and empty up as far as Mt. Auburn Hospital where it meandered west and out of sight. Downstream, looking left, it was spanned by the Western Avenue Bridge and the River Street Bridge before it meandered east near Boston University. The ice on the river still held, but the warmer weather would have its way and by late afternoon there would be water on top of the ice.

"Really—fans. They think they know you, and they are so insistent sometimes." Jill stared out the window of the Cherokee as she talked. They were shooting on location today, in the Waterfront Park near the Marriott Hotel. I turned east onto Soldiers Field Road in front of the Business School. Jill stared at the big snow-covered lawn and the red brick Georgian buildings in a self-important cluster around it.

"What's that?"

"Business School," I said.

"Which one?"

"Harvard Business School," I said. "There are people in there who would suffer dyspepsia if they heard you ask *which one.* They don't even use its abbreviated name. Mostly they call it the B School. Graduates platoons of people each year who are Captains of Industry at once."

"Don't sound so critical," Jill said as we slid under the Western Avenue overpass. "What are you captain of?"

"My soul," I said. "Who's the guy in the Lincoln?"

"Why won't you believe what I tell you," she said. "I probably met him at some reception when we were slugging the series, and he thinks he's in love with me."

"We'll see him again," I said.

"I'm sure you can take care of that," Jill said. "You certainly hit that other man hard enough."

"That guy's better than he looked," I said.

"How can you tell?"

"He was very confident. He was used to winning."

"Well, he certainly underestimated you," she said.

"Next time he won't."

10

FROM a pay phone on Atlantic Avenue, I called a guy I knew named Harry Dobson at the Registry of Motor Vehicles and got a name and address to go with the plate number I'd lifted from this morning's Lincoln Town Car: Stanley Rojack, Sheep Meadow Lane, Dover. Then I found Morrissey the detail cop and told him I had an errand.

"She'll be here all day," I said, "according to the call sheet."

" 'Less she gets into a funk and goes in her mobile home to cry," Morrissey said.

"In which case all you have to do is hang around outside," I said. "It's better than chasing some crack dancer up a dark alley."

"You got that right," Morrissey said.

It was bright along the waterfront the way it only is when the snow isn't dirty yet, and the sun is out, and the light reflected off the gray ocean and the white snow makes you squint. Even if you are wearing your Ray-Bans. This wasn't a working waterfront. This was a stockbrokers' and young lawyers' waterfront. The boats along the dock were sloops and Chris-Crafts, and the long gray granite warehouses had been turned into condominiums with sand-blasted brick interiors and bleached timbers showing. You could buy a blue margarita on ten seconds' notice down here.

I got my car from where I'd parked it back of the prop truck, next to a hydrant under a sign that said TOW ZONE. One of the nice things about working for a movie company, you could park in the mayor's office and people would just walk around your car and smile and say "Love the show."

I went along under the artery to the South Station Tunnel, and through, and bore right onto the Mass. Pike that cruised along the old railroad right-of-way through, and mostly below, the center of the city. We went under the Prudential Center, which was built on the old railroad yards, and on out past Fenway, and Boston University, past the old Braves Field with its bright ugly carpet of Astroturf, where once the grass had grown. In maybe fifteen minutes I hit 128 and headed south. The roads were thick with surly Christmas shoppers, but there were no shopping centers yet between the turnpike and the Dover exit, and the pace quickened. Route 128 was clear of snow, and the exits were fully plowed and clear. I didn't even need to put the Jeep in four-wheel drive. I rarely needed to put it in four-wheel drive. Sometimes I went out and drove around in snowstorms just to justify it. I took Route 109 and then Walpole Street and I was in Dover.

Dover is a WASP fantasy of the nineteenth century. The streets were arched with trees, bare black limbs now, crusted with snow, but in the summer effulgent with leaves. The houses were infrequent, and often invisible at the far end of winding driveways disguised as dirt roads. The architecture was white clapboard and the voters would probably have supported Caligula. Sheep Meadow Lane was at the far end of Walpole Street, curving off to the right among trees and bushes. Along each side was the kind of white three-board fence that you see around Lexington, Kentucky, and sure enough, pushing the snow aside and grazing below it were horses, oddly shaggy in their winter coats. Parts of the pasture looked like an old apple orchard with the squat trees misshapen in their leaflessness. In several stretches along the winding road, disheveled stone walls, superseded by the neat white fencing, ran parallel to it, no longer functional; now only quaint.

It was nearly 11:00 in the morning and the winter sun was warmer than it should have been. Moisture dripped from the trees, and the plowed road was glistening with snow melt. Around a turn was Rojack's house. It was one of those places that an architect had been given a free hand with, and too much money. He had decided that he could make a totally postmodern statement without violating the traditional forms implicit in the setting. The place looked like it had been designed by Georges Braque while drunk. It was slabs and angles and cubes and slants in fieldstone and brick and glass and timber, and it flaunted itself against the pastured landscape in self-satisfied excess. Beyond it the pasture land, studded with an occasional apple tree, rolled down toward a river. Horses moved about in the pasture. Beyond the horses and facing the pasture was a barn, newly built, that mimicked the old barns of New England the way fashion mimics clothing.

I parked in the big driveway that made a half-circle in front of the house. It was done in paving stones. Water dripped from the roofline of the house and made a pleasant winter sound as I walked up the sinuous brick path to the glass and redwood entryway. A wind chime at the entry made a small tinkle. I rang the bell. Wherever it rang in the house I couldn't hear it. But it worked because in a minute the door opened and there was the tall mean geek I had disagreed with earlier this morning. His eyes behind the rimless glasses were expressionless when he looked at me.

"What do you want?"

"I'm with Dover Welcome Wagon," I said. "I wanted to stop by and drop off some soap samples and the name of your nearest plumber."

He started to say *buzz off,* caught himself and changed it.

"Beat it," he said.

I took a card out of my shirt pocket and handed it to him.

"I lied about Welcome Wagon," I said.

"Don't get foolish because you were able to sucker punch me this morning. I've pulverized tougher guys than you."

His voice had a hard nasal sound to it, the old Yankee sound, and he talked like the class bully at Deerfield Academy. A tough WASP?

"Sure," I said. "I still need to talk with Rojack."

He wasn't sure. He didn't have authority to screen callers.

"Wait here," he said and closed the door in my face. I waited in the tinkling silence, listening to the wind chimes and the roof drip. Then he opened the door again.

"This way," he said. I stepped in. He closed the door behind me. The house inside was all angles and slants. I followed him through an open hallway that appeared to cut the house diagonally. Rooms full of glass and stone and costly furniture opened off it as we went. I got a glimpse of Oriental rugs and the kind of early-twentieth-century Mission Oak furniture from a factory in Syracuse that sells for $25,000 a couch. I also got the impression of a lot of Tiffany glass before I came out into an English conservatory, all glass, fully enclosed, heated, and furnished in white wicker with floral cushions.

Rojack sat on the wicker couch among some huge potted ferns. He was wearing a Black Watch plaid shirt open at the neck, pressed chino pants and mahogany-colored penny loafers with no socks. On the couch next to him was a stack of manila file folders. On the coffee table before him was a laptop computer, its screen aglow with printing. He was drinking coffee from a white china cup that had a gold strip around the rim, and there was a full coffee service in silver on the table next to the computer.

He was a good-looking man, short dark hair brushed straight back, dark expressive face. Medium sized, in shape. His nails glistened as he lowered the coffee cup and looked directly at me.

"A private detective," he said.

"Sad but true," I said.

"Randall's dying to throw you out," Rojack said.

"Why should he be different?"

Rojack nodded. "You are often unwelcome?"

"I often bring bad news," I said.

"That is usually unwelcome. Do you bring bad news to me?"

"No," I said. "I bring questions."

I felt like I was trapped in a Hemingway short story. If I got any more cryptic I wouldn't be able to talk at all.

Rojack nodded, carefully. It was as if everything he did he had learned to do.

"Sit down," he said. "Will you have coffee?"

"Yes, please. Cream, two sugars." Asking for decaf seemed somehow inappropriate.

Rojack nodded at Randall. Without expression he poured some coffee for me, added a splash of cream and two lumps of sugar, put a small silver spoon on the white saucer and handed the coffee to me. Outside, the bright pasture sloped away to the riverbank in the midday sunlight, while the water ran across the glass roof of the atrium in thick rivulets and dripped rhythmically down the sides. Somewhere in the house there was a wood fire burning. I could smell it. After he gave me the coffee, Randall stood back against the archway that led to the atrium and waited with his arms folded. He was wearing a white warm-up suit with a cobalt stripe down the arm and leg seams, and some sort of off-white canvas slippers. The zipper on the warm-up suit was down about halfway, and he appeared to be wearing a lisle tank top underneath. Without uncrossing his arms he inspected the nails on his right hand.

"What questions do you have for me, Mr. Spenser?"

"First let me tell you my situation," I said. I drank a little coffee. It was good. What's a little rapid heartbeat now and then.

"I have been employed to do a couple of things for Jill Joyce, the television star with whom you were trying to speak this morning."

Rojack nodded. Randall admired his nails. I sipped a bit more coffee.

"One," I said, "I'm supposed to protect her from harassment, hence my unkindness to old Randall here."

Rojack nodded again. Randall examined the nails on his left hand.

"Second," I said, "I'm supposed to find out who's harassing her."

We all paused.

"Hence, as it were, my visit here."

"You think I am harassing Jill Joyce?"

"No," I said. "I don't know what you are doing with Jill Joyce. But I need to know, in order to do what I was hired to do. So I thought I'd come out and ask."

"Even though you had reason to assume that Randall would be, ah, angry with you?"

"I can live with Randall's anger," I said.

Rojack smiled without any humor. "Perhaps," he said.

We all thought about that for a moment.

"What has Jill told you about our relationship?" Rojack said.

"She says she doesn't know you."

Rojack was too carefully practiced in his every mannerism to show surprise. But he was expressionless for a moment and I guessed that maybe my answer had affected him.

"She is a liar," Rojack said, finally.

"She certainly is," I said.

"What do you wish to know?"

"Anything," I said. "I can't get her to tell me her birthday. I don't even know enough to ask an intelligent question. Tell me anything about her, and it will be progress."

"She is a drunk," Rojack said.

"That I know."

"And, I don't know if the term is used anymore, a nymphomaniac."

"I don't think it is, but I know that too."

"She uses drugs."

"Yeah."

Rojack shrugged. "So what else is there to know?"

"How do you know her?" I said.

"At a cocktail party," Rojack said. "The governor had a party in the State House rotunda for the stars and top executives of *Fifty Minutes,* when it first came to town to shoot the pilot. Three years ago. I went—I am a substantial contributor to the governor's campaigns—and I met her there. I gave her a card. A couple of days later she called and said that she was alone in town, living in a hotel, and wanted someone to take her out and help her not be lonely."

Far down in the pasture, at the edge of the stream, one of the horses put his head down and drank. He was a red roan horse, and he made an ornamental contrast to the white pasture and the black trees, blacker than usual with the snow melt glistening on their sides.

"I was pleased—most men would be. I took her to dinner at L'Espalier. We had wine. We went to the Plaza Bar. We came home here . . ." Rojack made a shrugging hand-spread gesture; among us men of the world, it would be clear what happened next.

"So you were going steady?"

"I don't enjoy your manner very much, Spenser."

"Damn," I said. "Everybody says that. Did you and Jill Joyce spend a lot of time together?"

"We were intimate for several years. Then she stopped seeing me."

"Why?"

"I don't know. I had done her several favors. Perhaps once they were accomplished she felt no further need of me."

"Tell me about the favors," I said. My cup was

empty. I put it down on the coffee table. Automatically Rojack picked up a small napkin from the coffee service tray and put it under my saucer.

"Some were merely routine: reservations at a restaurant, tickets for a sold-out event, a drunken driving charge—I have a good deal of influence."

"Congratulations. Were there any favors that weren't routine?"

Rojack leaned back thoughtfully and gazed out at his trees and horses. He looked healthy and very satisfied. He was talking about himself, and he took it seriously.

"I suppose one must define routine," Rojack said.

I waited.

"There was a somewhat salacious piece of gossip that I was able to keep out of the papers."

I waited.

"It involved a young driver on the show and Jill in an elevator."

I nodded encouragingly. There was no need to prod him. He liked talking about the things he could fix. He'd tell me all there was. Maybe more.

"And there was a young man whom she'd known before she went to Hollywood."

Rojack said *Hollywood* the way a lot of people did, as if it were a place where one might actually run into Carole Lombard on any corner. As if it were glamorous. The sun had edged up to its low winter zenith as we'd sat talking, and now it shone directly in on the atrium from above and reflected in whitely from the unlittered snow. Everything shone with great clarity.

"Apparently this young man had been calling Jill, trying to see her, and Jill wanted nothing to do with him. But he persisted until Jill spoke to me about it, and I sent Randall to ask him to stop."

"And he stopped?" I said.

"Randall can be very convincing," Rojack said.

Leaning on the archway, Randall looked as pleased with himself as Rojack did. He was one of those raw-boned, square-shouldered Yankee types with long muscles and big knuckley hands—all angles and planes, as if he'd been designed to go with the house.

"What's this guy's name?" I said.

Rojack looked at Randall.

"Pomeroy," Randall said. "Wilfred Pomeroy."

"Where's he live?"

"Place out in Western Mass., Waymark, one of those Berkshire hill towns."

"Waymark?"

"Un huh."

"What was Jill's connection to him?"

Rojack pursed his lips for a moment. "Pelvic," he said.

I nodded.

"So," I said, "why were you after her this morning?"

Rojack picked up his coffee cup, saw that it was empty, gestured toward Randall with it. Randall came over, took it, filled it, put it back. During which time I watched the red roan horse browse beneath the soft snow.

Randall took a sip of coffee. He held the cup in both hands, like people do in coffee commercials, and then they say *ahhh!* He didn't say *ahhh!* He stared for a moment into the cup and then he raised his eyes.

"We agree," he said, "that Jill has many failings."

I nodded. At the end of the pasture, the red roan browsed too close to a chestnut with a red mane. The chestnut stretched out its neck and took a nip at the roan. The roan shied, kicked at the chestnut, and moved away. The peaceable kingdom.

"But what you probably don't see is the Jill that is so . . ." He searched thoughtfully for the right adjective. He spoke as if every word were being reported to an eager world. "Compelling," he said. "When she is intimate with you she is totally intimate, she is completely yours and her . . ." Again he examined a choice of several words, turning them over the way a housewife buys fruit. "Her aura is so enveloping . . . it's quite hypnotic."

"So when she dumps you it's hard to believe," I said.

"And harder still to accept," Rojack said.

"You tried calling, and stopping by, and such."

"Without success," Rojack said.

"So you thought you'd get her early, and you brought Randall along to help you reason with her."

"I always bring Randall along, everywhere," Rojack said.

"You been calling her anonymously, sending scary messages?"

"No. I've called her, yes; but she knew it was me, and she always hung up on me. The calls were not . . . criminal. I have written her, but again, there was nothing of an harassing nature."

He actually said "an harassing."

"You haven't threatened her?"

"No."

"Dirty tricks of any kind?"

"Spenser, I am a man who does not find any need to resort to dirty tricks."

"Too important for stuff like that," I said.

"Quite simply," Rojack said, "yes."

We sat wordlessly for a moment or two in the sun-flooded glass room.

"Anything else you can tell me about Jill?" I said.

Rojack shook his head.

"Sort of funny," I said. "She got you to chase Wilfred away. Now she's got me to chase you away."

"I don't plan to be chased away, Spenser. I am not a man who is used to being *dumped,* as you put it."

Again the sunny silence. I shrugged. And stood.

"You seem very physical, Spenser. Do you work out?"

"Some," I said.

"Perhaps I can show you our gym, before you go. Perhaps," Rojack smiled, a formal gesture of self-deprecation, as sincere as a congressman's hand-shake, "I can impress you."

"Sure," I said.

Rojack stood and let me out of the atrium. Randall followed.

11

THE gym was better than the Harbor Health Club, except Henry Cimoli wasn't there. It had a full Nautilus setup, a complete set of York barbells, some parallel bars, some rings, a treadmill, a stair climber, jump ropes, a heavy bag, a speed bag. There was a lap pool off the gym part, and a sauna and steam and massage setup between the two. The walls of the gym were mirrored. The floor was done in some sort of resilient rubber padding. There were fluorescent lights recessed in a textured ceiling, and there were skylights through which the bright blue sky glistened.

"Zowie," I said.

"Randall," Rojack said, "perhaps you'd like to show Spenser how some of the equipment works."

"I know how it works," I said.

Nobody paid any attention. Randall shucked off his warm-up jacket and stepped out of his canvas shoes. His bare feet were white and bony with long toes and a tuft of hair on each instep. There were many distended veins in his pale arms, and the knobby muscles knotted and slacked as he moved. He jumped off the ground, caught the rings that hung straight down from the ceiling, and proceeded to do a series of gymnastic loops and frolics on them that were pretty impressive for a guy who looked to be about six feet four. He dismounted with a somersault and launched an all-out karate attack on the heavy bag, spinning in midair to kick it, whirling balletically to drive home an elbow or a sharp-knuckled fist. His movements were sometimes too quick to follow and the heavy bag pitched and shivered as he hit it, kicked it, slashed it, and butted it, all at what appeared to be the speed of sound. For the *coup de grace* he leaped into the air, scissor-kicked the bag with both feet and went into a backward somersault as he landed on his back, rolling to his feet in one continuous motion. He was breathing hard and his pale angular body was glistening with sweat as he stood erect, almost at attention, still wearing his rimless glasses, his flat blue eyes fixed on me. Rojack looked at him like the father of an Eagle Scout.

"That kind of thing happen to you often?" I said.

Rojack said, "We both felt it important that you understand about Randall, that you recognize clearly that this morning was merely a very lucky misjudgment on Randall's part . . . lucky, that is, for you."

Randall was so thrilled by his performance that his face was fluorescent with excitement.

"Is he going to do anything else?" I said. "Juggle four steak knives while whistling 'Malaguena'? Something like that?"

Randall's breath was still coming a little short.

"You like to . . . show us . . . what *you* . . . can do on the bag?"

I looked at Rojack.

"Be my guest," he said. I think the sound in his voice was mockery.

"Go ahead . . . big shot," Randall said.

I shrugged, reached under my left shoulder, pulled my gun and put a bullet into the middle of the body bag. The sound of the shot was shockingly loud in the silent gym. The body bag jumped. I put the gun back under my arm, smiled in a friendly way at Rojack and Randall, and walked out. As I headed through the house to the front door, the smell of the pistol shot lingered gently after me.

12

THE next day was Saturday and Jill wasn't working so Susan and I took her to sightsee. Susan was a little annoyed that she had to share her weekend with Jill Joyce, and when I thoughtfully pointed out to her that I wouldn't be stuck guarding Jill's body in the first place if it weren't for Susan, she didn't seem any happier.

I was in the lobby when hotel security brought her down. She was wearing a pink cashmere workout suit, and white, high-topped, leather aerobic shoes with pink and white laces. She carried her black mink over her arm, her copper-blond hair glistened as if fresh from a hundred brush strokes, and her face looked as fresh and innocent as Daisy Duck's. She hit the security guy with a smile so radiant that he'd probably have thrown himself on his sword, if she'd asked. If he'd had a sword.

"Well, my incredible hulk," she said. "Where will you take me today?"

"Wherever you want to go," I said. "Within reason."

Jill linked her arm through mine. "Lead on, Macbeth," she said.

We went out to where Susan was waiting in the

Cherokee. The windows were tinted and Jill didn't know that Susan was there until I opened the back door for Jill and she stopped and shook her head.

"I'll ride up front," she said.

"Front's taken," I said.

The side window went down and Susan smiled out at Jill.

"You remember Susan Silverman," I said.

"I didn't know she'd be here," Jill said to me.

"We try to spend most weekends together," I said. "When we can."

"Spenser's Boston tour has become legendary," Susan said. "I think you'll enjoy it."

"You've been hired to protect me," Jill said to me.

"I know. Susan's going to work free," I said.

"Hop in, Jill." Susan was jollier than two yule logs.

I held the back door open, and after a short pause Jill got in. I went around, got behind the wheel, and off we went. Jill sat stiffly upright in the back seat. Susan shifted around so that she could see both Jill and me when she spoke.

"Have you gotten to see much of Boston since you've been here, Jill?" Susan asked.

"No."

"What a shame. It really is a lovely city."

"You try to get out when you're working sixteen hours a day every day, and some lunatic is threatening your life," Jill said.

"That must be very trying," Susan said. Her voice was sympathetic, but to the accomplished listener, and I'd been listening closely to Susan since 1974, there was humor and maybe the edge of something else in there.

"You got that right, sister."

We went along the river and pulled off on Charles Street. I found a convenient No-Parking-Here-To-Corner opening and pulled in near the recycled Universalist Meeting House.

"Charles Street," I said.

"We did a scene down here, somewhere, in an old firehouse," Jill said.

It was still warm. The brick sidewalks on Charles Street were wet with the puddled snow melt, and every eave dripped. There were Christmas trees being sold on the corner of Chestnut Street, and a Salvation Army Santa rang his bell in front of Toscano Restaurant.

"'Tis the season to be jolly," I said.

"So," Jill said, "it's Susan, isn't it?"

Susan nodded.

"Aren't you on the show in some way or other?"

"Yes," Susan said with a big sunny smile. "I'm the technical consultant."

We were walking toward the Common. The crowds on Charles Street were in the spirit of the season. People were angry and sullen and tired as they shoved past each other carrying shopping bags. Sweaty in their winter clothing, they packed into the small trendy shops and bumped each other with their packages.

"What's that mean?" Jill said.

Susan was wearing a black leather jacket and black jeans. The jeans were tucked into some low-heeled soft leather cobalt boots that wrinkled fashionably around her ankles. Next to her Jill Joyce looked maybe just a trifle silly.

"I'm a psychotherapist," Susan said, "and I offer suggestions to make the show more authentic."

"You're a shrink?"

"Un huh."

"You're a doctor?"

"I have a Ph.D. in psychology."

We reached the corner of Beacon Street.

"Up to the left," I said, "is the State House. That's the Common there, and on the other side of Charles is the Public Garden."

The trees on the Common were strung with Christmas lights. It was bright with them at night, though it was hard to see now. The Common was snow covered, and full of people crisscrossing its walks in bright clothing. At a distance they looked cheery. The white snow and the dark trees made a bright contrast to the predominant red brick tones of Beacon Hill that rose along our side of the Common and slanted down Park Street behind it. The steeple of the Park Street Church gestured over the rise of the Common, against the blue winter sky. Two hundred years ago they'd hidden gunpowder in its cellar.

"I want a drink," Jill said.

"I can see why," I said. "It's nearly three hours since breakfast."

"I don't give a fuck what time it is," Jill said. "When I feel like a drink I feel like a drink."

"Want some lunch with that?" I said.

"Maybe I do, maybe I don't," Jill said.

We walked across the Public Garden to the new Four Seasons Hotel and sat at a table near the bar. Jill had a glass of white wine. Susan and I had club soda. Jill drank a gulp of white wine, took out a cigarette and leaned toward me. I didn't have a match and there weren't any on the table. I shrugged and spread my hands.

Jill said, "We'll get some from the waitress."

The waitress spotted our dilemma and brought over a book of matches before I could ask her. I took them and lit Jill's cigarette. Jill took a long drag, exhaled, swallowed some more wine. The bar was nearly empty at twenty to noon. It was sprawling and low with many sofas and little tables. The lighting was dim. There were times when a quiet bar early in the day is nearly perfect. Jill finished her wine.

"Get me another," she said.

"No. I perform heroic feats if you are threatened. But I don't fetch things."

"You get me one," she said and pointed her chin at Susan.

"I'll see if I can get the waitress," Susan said pleasantly.

Again the waitress was alert. She had nothing else to do. And she was over with Jill's second wine almost at once.

"So." Jill had a third of her second glass inside her.

She sprawled back in her chair and rested her head and looked along her nose at me. "You don't fetch things."

I shook my head.

"You usually bring your girlfriend along when you're protecting someone?"

"If she'll come," I said.

Jill got that crafty, you-have-fallen-in-my-trap look that drunks get at the right point in their drinking.

"So if someone tries to kill us, who will you protect first?" she said.

"Susan," I said.

Jill started to speak and stopped and stared at me.

"You son of a bitch," she said, finally, and drank the rest of her wine. The waitress knew she had a live one and was right there for the refill.

"The point is it isn't likely to work out that way," I said. "I don't think someone will try to kill *us.* If there's trouble, it will be directed at you. Susan will get out of the way, and I'll explode into action."

"But you'd save her first, ahead of me?"

"Yeah."

Jill twirled her wineglass slowly by the stem. Now that she had some in her, and more available, she could afford to take it slow. Her eyes were fixed on me. Susan sat quietly, listening, interested as she always was about everything. Two couples with plaid pants and cameras came into the bar and sat at the far side from us. One of the women looked over and whispered to her husband and they stared over.

Then the other two stared. One of the men nodded. The other man said something and all four of them laughed. One of the women slapped her husband's hand as she laughed.

Jill twirled her wineglass a little.

"Well," she said finally, "I guess I know where I stand."

I saw something change in Susan's face.

"Jill," she said, "this whole conversation is inane."

"Excuse me?" Jill said.

"You're not worrying about who he'll protect. You're mad because you thought you'd have him to yourself today and instead, I showed up and spoiled it."

"Well, thank you, Dr. Ruth," Jill said.

"From your point of view I'm an intruder," Susan said. "I understand that. But that's because you have personalized the relationship. If you see it as a professional endeavor, in which he protects you because he's hired to, then the sense of intrusion goes away."

Jill stared at her for a moment. She drank some of her wine. Then she said, "Fuck you."

Susan nodded thoughtfully.

"Interesting point," she said. "Let me put this another way. Since Spenser was hired to protect you, you have been trying every way you can to climb into his lap, and I came along today so that if you tried it again I could kick your fat little butt out into Park Square."

Jill's eyes widened.

"Fat?" she said.

"Fat," Susan said, "and, if I may say so, gone south a little."

Jill began to breathe faster, her eyes still very wide. Tears formed and began to roll down her face.

"You are through," she said. "Both of you are not going to work on my goddamned show again."

"Curses," I said.

"Take me home," Jill said. "Now."

It was a strained and sullen trip back to the Charles Hotel. Jill sat in the back in haughty silence and smoked cigarettes which she lit herself, in a kind of self-imposed martyrdom. She got out when we got there and stalked into the hotel without a word. I drifted along behind her to make sure security was alert. They were. A guy picked her up in the lobby and went up with her in the elevator.

Back in the car I looked at Susan.

"I knew you'd get her to see it our way," I said.

"I shouldn't have lost my temper at her. But . . ." Susan shrugged.

"Hard not to," I said.

"And that damned coquettish Czarina act that she does with you . . ."

I nodded. We were cruising along Memorial Drive, heading into town, with the river on our right.

"What would you like to do now?" I said.

"Let's go to your place. You make a fire. I'll make a lunch. We'll open a bottle of wine and see what transpires."

"I'm pretty sure I know what will transpire," I said.

"No fair," Susan said. "You're a trained detective."

I nodded and turned right onto the Western Avenue Bridge.

"I don't think her fanny is fat," I said.

Susan smiled, the way she does when her face lights up and her eyes get brighter, and you know just what she looked like when she was sixteen.

"All's fair in love and war," she said.

13

I PICKED Jill up Monday morning and took her to the studio as if I hadn't been fired. She made no mention of Saturday. It had begun to snow late Sunday night and there was about three inches of soft feathery snow accumulated with no sign of slowing. I had the Cherokee in four-wheel drive and drove with the arrogance that only a man in a four-wheel-drive vehicle can feel. The California guys at the studio were all bundled up like Admiral Byrd as they stumbled around the studio parking lot.

The drivers were gathered in fur-trimmed parkas, holding coffee in thick-gloved hands and kibitzing in the cafeteria downstairs. I followed Jill to the wardrobe office. The door was ajar, and we went in. There was no one there.

"Kathleen?" Jill called. "Ernie?"

The lights were on. The clothing for costuming hung in neat order on pipe racks, filling most of the room. There was a counter to one side and an open space with mirrors, a cutting table, and an ironing board. On the counter was a glass jar of hard candies. I took a red one, hoping for cherry. It was raspberry. Even for the discerning palate, however, in hard candies the difference was but slight.

Jill said, "Spenser."

I turned and saw what she saw. Behind the counter, facedown on the floor, was a woman's body. The white blouse she was wearing was darkly blotched with dried blood.

I went around the corner and knelt. I knew she was dead. Checking her pulse was just a formality. Her skin was cold when I touched it. There was no pulse. There hadn't been for some hours. The woman's head was turned left, and the side of her face that showed was blank and meaningless. Her hair was the same coppery color that Jill's was.

I stood. Jill was standing very still. Her hands, clasped together so hard her knuckles were white, were pressed against her lips.

"You know who this is?" I said.

"I don't want to look," Jill said. She kept her hands pressed against her mouth as she spoke.

"I don't blame you," I said. "But one glance, please."

I walked around the counter and put my arm around her shoulders and moved her gently to where she could see the body. She kept her eyes closed.

"Okay," I said. "It's not that bad, just a look at her face, then you won't have to look again."

Jill opened her eyes, stared down for a moment over her clasped hands. Then she clamped her eyes shut again, very tightly.

"Oh, Jesus," she said softly. "Oh, Jesus."

"Who is it?" I said.

"Babe," she said. "Babe Loftus, my stunt double."

There didn't seem anything to say. I squeezed her a little tighter with my arm around her shoulders. She let her arms drop and turned her head in against my chest. We stood that way for a moment. There was a phone on the counter. Still holding on to Jill, I reached out and got it and punched in a number I knew too well by now.

A radio car showed up about two minutes after I called, and the two prowlies in it came in, looked things over, and were as careful as civilians not to touch things.

"You got a detail officer on this deal," one of the cops said.

"Ray Morrissey," I said.

"Tommy," the cop said to his partner, "whyn't you go and see if you can round him up."

The partner left.

I said, "I'll take Miss Joyce to her mobile home."

"No," she said, "Sandy's office."

She had her face still buried against my chest.

"Upstairs," I said, "in the line producer's office."

"Be sure to stay there. Homicide don't like it when they get here and the witnesses aren't around."

"We'll be there," I said.

Everybody looked stiff and uneasy as we passed through the corridor and up the main stairs to Salzman's office. The two women in the outer office were both on their feet at the top of the stairs looking down.

"Somebody said it was Babe," one of the women said.

I nodded. We went into Salzman's office. He wasn't there. He was on his way in.

Jill sank into one of the leather armchairs near Salzman's desk. Outside the picture windows the snow came steadily in wide pleasant flakes, drifting as it fell, but falling with the kind of purposeful steadiness that means business. Traffic was very slow on Soldiers Field Road. Cars had their headlights on in the gray daylight and the lights made a weak glow through the snow that accumulated on the headlight lenses. Wipers made dark rhomboids on the windshields, and beyond, winding through the white landscape, the river was icy black. The snow came thick enough so you couldn't see the other bank of the river.

Jill and I sat very quietly while we waited. That someone had shot Jill's stunt double didn't have to be connected to the threats and scary phone calls that Jill had been getting. But you could make a pretty good case that it might be, and you couldn't assume it was not.

After about twenty minutes Belson came into the office. He had his tan trench coat on with the collar up. The coat was unbuttoned. The tweed scally cap he was wearing was tilted down over the bridge of his nose so he had to tilt his head back a little to see. He stopped inside the front door when he entered and put his hands in the hip pockets of his pants.

You could see where he had his gun holstered inside his belt.

"Good day for it," Belson said. He had one of his ugly little cigars in the corner of his mouth.

I introduced Jill. Jill raised her eyes slowly from her lap and fixed Belson with a tragic stare.

"Oh, Frank," Jill said. "It's my stunt double."

If Belson minded being called *Frank* by a murder witness, he didn't let it show.

"You discovered the body," he said.

I said yes.

"Together?"

"Yes."

Belson nodded. As he spoke his eyes moved around the room, filing everything. Three months from now he would be able to describe the place in exact detail.

"I talked with Morrissey," Belson said.

"So you know what I'm doing here," I said.

Belson nodded again. He pushed a couple of items away from the corner of Salzman's desk and sat on it, one leg dangling, one leg still on the floor.

"Your usual bang-up job," Belson said.

"Maybe you should follow me around on this one," I said. "Learn as you go."

"For God's sake," Jill said. "Don't you people realize what happened? That was meant for me. He thought Babe was me."

"Who thought that?" Belson said.

"There's a man," Jill said. "He's been threatening

me, saying terrible things. Now he's done this. He thought Babe was me."

"What's his name?" Belson said.

"I don't know. That's what he's supposed to find out." Jill jerked her head at me. "Only he hasn't found out anything, and now he's tried to kill me."

"Spenser?"

"No, no. The man."

Sandy Salzman came into the office wearing a down parka and moon boots. He went straight to Jill Joyce.

"Jill, honey, are you okay?"

"Better than Babe Loftus," I said.

"Oh my God, Babe," Salzman said. "What happened?"

"We're looking into that," Belson said.

"Are you the police?"

"I'm one of them," Belson said. He flipped out his shield. "Belson," he said. "Homicide."

Salzman was holding Jill Joyce's hand. She put her other hand over his and laid her head against his arm.

"Sandy, please, get me out of here," Jill said.

Salzman looked at Belson.

Belson said, "Where's she going to go?"

"Charles Hotel," Salzman said.

"We can locate that," Belson said. "We may want to talk with her."

"I think we should have an attorney present," Salzman said.

"Of course," Belson said. "Important person like her. Probably ought to have two or three present."

"No need to be unpleasant," Salzman said. "I just think with a star of Jill's magnitude it's prudent."

Belson looked at me and something that might have been amusement showed for a moment in his thin face.

"This one's going to be a good time," he said.

"I'm taking Miss Joyce to the hotel," Salzman said. "Feel free to use my office."

"You want Cambridge to send somebody over to keep an eye out?" Belson said. "Now that there's a homicide involved."

"Yes," Salzman said. "And the hotel security staff is alerted."

"Fine," Belson said. "I'll want Spenser for an hour or so."

Salzman was already guiding Jill out of his office. She looked back at me.

"You'll come, won't you?" she said. "You'll stay with me?"

"I'll be along," I said.

They left the room. Belson got up and closed the door behind them and walked across to the big picture window and stood looking out at the snow. His cigar had gone out some time ago, as it almost always did. He lit it with a kitchen match that he scratched on the window sill. Outside the pleasant snow came steadily down. Belson turned from the window, folded his arms, leaned against the sill.

"What do you think?" he said.

"I don't know," I said. "I haven't known since I got involved. I never more than half believed there was anyone harassing her."

"Tell me about it," Belson said.

I did. When I was through Belson took the little cigar, now down to a stub, from his mouth and pursed his lips.

"This thing is going to be a hair ball."

I nodded.

"M.E. show up yet?" I said.

"Not while I was there. She looks to have been shot twice in the back with a big gun. Three fifty-seven maybe. Been dead awhile. No sign of a struggle. Nobody we've talked to so far has heard anything. Nobody so far knows why she would have been in here on a Sunday night."

"Even if she were, why would the murderer be here?" I said. "If he was after Jill he wouldn't expect to find her here."

"Maybe he was after the victim, and maybe he came with her."

"Or brought her," I said.

Belson had the cigar back in his mouth. He rolled it directly into the center of his mouth and talked around it.

"Why would he bring her?"

"Maybe it wasn't mistaken identity," I said. "Maybe it was a sign, more harassment, like the hanged Jill Joyce doll."

Belson nodded. "Or maybe it's all a fake. Maybe the whole Jill Joyce harassment is to make us think the wrong thing, and the murderer really just wanted to kill this stunt woman."

"Babe Loftus," I said.

"Yeah."

"Possible," I said. "Kind of bizarre, though."

"Like your scenario isn't?" Belson said.

I shrugged.

"Where's Quirk?" I said. "This is a hot enough squeal to bring him out."

Belson showed no expression. He had one of those permanent five o'clock shadows that no razor could successfully obliterate.

"Command staff meeting," Belson said. "Strategies for improving police/community interface."

"Honest to God?" I said.

"Honest to God."

14

JILL looked at Hawk the way a mackerel eyes a minnow.

"Well," she said as Hawk walked across the Quiet Bar at the Charles. He had on black cowboy boots and an ankle-length black leather trench coat. The coat was open, the collar up, and a black turtleneck showed at the throat. His skin was maybe half a shade lighter than the leather coat, and his smooth head gleamed in the bar's indirect lighting.

"You just wear those boots to be taller than me," I said.

"Taller than you anyway," Hawk said.

"Are not," I said.

"Better-looking, too," Hawk said.

"Aren't you going to introduce us?" Jill Joyce said.

I did. Jill was sitting on a couch quietly, but as she looked at Hawk she seemed somehow to wiggle without moving.

"Well," she said, "aren't you something."

"Un huh," Hawk said.

He sat on the couch beside Jill. The waitress appeared eagerly.

"Laphroig," Hawk said, "straight, in a lowball glass."

"Yes, sir," the waitress said and hurried off on her mission. She placed her order at the service end of the bar and glanced back at Hawk while she waited.

"Why didn't you tell me about him," Jill said to me.

"I did. I told you he would look out for you while I was away and that he was almost as good as I was, and better than anyone else."

"But you didn't mention . . ." Jill spread her hands in a *voilà* gesture at Hawk.

"She means you didn't tell her about me being a sexual icon."

"You're right," I said. "I didn't tell her that."

"Are you almost as good as he is?" Jill said. Like most things she said, it was larded with innuendo.

"Better," Hawk said.

"Really?" Jill's eyes were wide and excited. "The other day he knocked down a great tall man, bing! bing! just like that." Jill made two darling little punching movements.

"Just like that?" Hawk said.

"More or less," I said.

The waitress brought Hawk's scotch and another white wine for Jill. They had learned her habits here and seemed to have mastered the technique of keeping her glass filled.

"Can you do that?" Jill asked. She smiled at him, a *TV Guide* cover smile, over the rim of her wineglass and drank a bit.

"Don't know about bing! bing!" Hawk said.

Jill reached over and squeezed Hawk's biceps. A

moment of genuine surprise popped for only a moment into her eyes before the flirty TV-star cuteness slipped back in place.

"Whooooa," she said.

Hawk stared at me.

"Pay's excellent," I said.

Hawk nodded. "Good to remember that," he said.

Jill slugged back most of the rest of her wine.

"So here's how it's going to work," I said. "Hawk will take care of you at work and to and from. Cambridge P.D. will have a car here from six at night to six in the morning. Hotel security will watch your room. They'll be connected to the prowlies by radio."

"Prowlies?" Jill said. She was glancing toward the bar. The waitress started toward her with another glass of wine, and I could see the tension ease as Jill spotted her.

"Police car," I said.

The waitress put the wine down. Jill picked it up, took a genteel sip.

"You want to go out nights, or whatever, you arrange it with Hawk."

"And will he go out with me?"

"That's for you and him to work out."

"Will you?" Jill leaned toward Hawk as she spoke. The throat of her simple white blouse was open and as she leaned forward there was a clear line of cleavage.

"Sure," he said.

"And I, meanwhile, will chase down whoever has been annoying you and urge them to stop," I said.

"Can you find him?"

"Sure," I said.

"How?"

"You start looking," I said. "And you ask people things, and then that leads you to somebody else and you ask them and they tell you something that hooks you into somebody, and so on."

"But where on earth will you start?"

She had a little trouble with the separation between *earth* and *will.*

"I already have," I said. "I started with your friend Rojack."

She frowned. She took a drink. She frowned again.

"I told you I don't know him."

"Know his name though," I said.

" 'Course I know his name."

"He says you and he were an item."

"He's a creep," Jill said.

"Is there anything you'd like to add to that appraisal?"

Hawk sat quietly. Now and then he took a small taste of his scotch. He watched Jill's behavior happily, as if he'd paid a modest admission fee and felt he'd gotten a bargain.

"I don't want to talk about him," Jill said.

"You think he did it?" I said.

Jill shook her head angrily.

"I'll find it out anyway," I said. "Wouldn't it

make sense to tell me what you know, and get it over with quicker?"

"I'm hungry," Jill said.

I slid the bowl of smokehouse almonds toward her. She took a handful and ate them silently, then drank some more wine. She had turned away from me as she did so and was eyeing Hawk.

"You married?" she said.

Hawk shook his head.

"Got anybody?" Jill said.

"Lots," Hawk said.

"I mean anybody special," Jill said.

"They all special," Hawk said.

"You like white girls?"

Hawk looked at me again.

"Tell me 'bout that pay again?" he said.

"Good. It's good as hell," I said. "And you get a free watermelon, too."

Hawk nodded. Jill bored in on him.

"Do you?"

"Not stupid," Hawk said. "Mostly I prefer not stupid."

"Did Spenser tell you what I've been looking for ever since I got to Boston?" She put an *h* in *Boston.*

"A noble black savage," Hawk said.

Jill shook her head. She was implacable. She probably didn't listen to what I said or Hawk said or the byplay between us.

"I want something about this long," she said and made her two-foot measuring gesture again.

Hawk examined the distance between her hands seriously, then nodded thoughtfully.

"Could send over my little brother," he said.

15

HAWK was still nursing his first Laphroig, I was two-thirds through my first Sam Adams, and Jill was just beginning her fifth white wine.

"Before you doze off," I said, "can we talk about Wilfred Pomeroy?"

Jill had no reaction for a moment, then she looked very carefully up from under her lowered gaze and said to me, "Who?"

"Wilfred Pomeroy. Rojack says he was harassing you and had to be chased away."

"I don't know anything about it," she said.

"As far as I can tell, Jill, you don't know anyone and you've never done anything. Why would Rojack make up a story about Wilfred Pomeroy?"

"Rojack's a creep."

"Who could think up a name like Wilfred Pomeroy?" I said.

"Who cares about Pomeroy?" Jill said. "Why are you bothering me with all these creeps?"

There were two well-groomed young women in tailored suits sitting on the next couch. They both wore very high heels and they both were sipping Gibsons. Everything about them said, *We have MBAs.*

"This is called detecting," I said. "I'm trying to find out who murdered your stunt double, in the hopes that I can dissuade him, or her, from murdering you."

Hawk had leaned back in the couch and crossed his feet on the cocktail table. He held the single-malt scotch in both hands and rested it on a point above his solar plexus. He was examining the two MBAs with calm interest, the way one examines a painting.

"Her?"

"Could be a her, couldn't it?"

"Why would any woman want to kill me? I don't even know any women."

"You know Wilfred Pomeroy?"

"No."

One of the MBAs had become aware of Hawk's gaze. She kept looking back at him in covert ways: pretending to glance out the window, casually surveying the room. She murmured something to her friend, who leaned forward to put her drink down and peeked at Hawk from under her bangs. Hawk continued to examine them without any reaction to their behavior.

"And Rojack's lying?" I said.

"Yes," Jill said. She had some wine.

"But you have no idea why he would tell lies like this?"

"No."

I leaned back and rested my head against the back of the couch and drummed my fingers lightly on the tops of my thighs. Jill had some wine.

Hawk said, "Hard to imagine why anyone want to harass her, isn't it?"

I rolled my head a little to the left so I could look at Hawk.

"Hard," I said.

"Susan met her?" Hawk said.

"Yes."

"She a suspect?"

I grinned.

"She has motive," I said.

Jill was savoring her wine. She seemed capable of not hearing any conversation she didn't want to hear.

"Are you a detective too?" she said to Hawk.

Hawk's smile was radiant. He shook his head.

"Well, what do you do?"

"Mostly what I feel like," Hawk said.

"But, I mean, do you protect people all the time?"

Again the big smile from Hawk.

"Nope," he said. "Sometimes I'm on the other side."

Jill looked at me.

I shrugged.

"I didn't say he was nice. I said he was good."

"I don't think either one of you is very nice," Jill said. Her voice was very small and girlish.

"Maybe," Hawk said to me, "we should can this job and protect those two."

He nodded at the MBAs. Jill looked at them.

"I could show you some things that those two tight asses don't know between them."

"Good to know," Hawk said.

16

In the morning I headed west on the Mass. Pike with the sun gleaming off the new snow and the temperature in the low thirties. I felt good. I'd looked up Waymark on the map and it was there. It was as close as I'd gotten to a clue in this whole deal. For the first time since I'd met Jill Joyce, I knew where I was going.

Waymark was in the Berkshire Hills, maybe two hours and twenty minutes west of Boston. There was a high gloss of rustic chic in the Berkshires, Tanglewood, Stockbridge, Williamstown Theater Festival; and there were enclaves of rural poverty where the official town mascot was probably a rat. Waymark was one of those. Driving into the east end of town after a long winding climb out of the valley, I saw a small house with a porch sagging across the length of the front and a discarded toilet bowl with a ratty Christmas tree stuck in it. In the next lot was a trailer, set on cinder blocks, its front yard fenced with bald tires, set in the ground to form a series of half-circles, black against the snow. Two brown cows, their ribs showing, stood silently at a wire fence and gazed at me as I rolled by, and in a yard next to a convenience store a milk goat was tethered to the wheel of a broken tractor.

Beside the convenience store, which advertised Orange Crush on an old-time sign that rose vertically beside the door, was a tall narrow two-story house with roofing shingles for siding. The shingles were a faded mustard color. Like a lot of the houses out here, it had a full veranda across the front. The veranda roof sagged in the middle enough so that the snow melt dripped off in the middle and puddled in front of the broken front step. There was a sign done in black house paint on a piece of one-by-ten pine board. TUNNYS GRILL it said. In front, on what once might have been a lawn, a couple of cars were parked nose in. I pulled in beside them. The space hadn't been cleared, merely rutted down by cars parking and backing out. I could see where some of them had gotten stuck and spun big hollows with their rear wheels. The dark earth below had been spun up onto the snow, mixing with exhaust soot and litter. I nosed in beside a vintage 1970 Buick and parked and got out. From Tunnys Grill came the odor of winter vegetables cooking—cabbage maybe, or turnips. I walked across the buckling wooden porch and in through a hollow-core luan door that was probably intended to go on the closet in a housing development ranch. It was not meant to be an outside door and the veneer was blistering and the color had faded to a pale gray brown. When I pushed it open the coarse smell of cooking was more aggressive.

Inside was a lightless corridor with a stairwell running up along the right wall to a closed door at the top. In front of the stairway to the right was an archway that had probably led into the living room. It had been closed off with a couple of pieces of plywood. Whoever had done it was an inexpert carpenter. Several of the nails were bent over, and instead of butting in the middle, one sheet of plywood lapped over the other. To the left was a similar archway, this one still open, and in what must once have been a dining room was a bar. There was a brown linoleum floor, three unmatched tables and some kitchen chairs, and a bar which had been worked up out of two long folding tables, the kind they use in church halls, with some red-checkered oilcloth tacked over it. Behind the bar was a tall dirty old refrigerator and some shelves with bottles on them. One shelf contained a row of unmatched glasses sitting mouth down on a folded dish towel. There was an old railroad wood stove set in a sandbox in the far corner opposite the bar, and on the wall to the left of the bar was a big florid picture of Custer's Last Stand, with a very Errol Flynnesque Custer standing, the last man upright, in the center of his fallen troop, his blond hair blowing in the wind of battle, firing a long pistol at the circling Indians.

There were two overweight guys in overalls and down vests sitting together near the stove drinking highballs and smoking cigarettes. The stove was putting out enough heat to bake bread, but both men seemed not to notice. They had on woolen shirts under the vests, and the sleeves of long underwear showed where they had turned their cuffs back. One of them had on a red woolen watch cap and the other a "Day-Glo" orange hunting cap with imitation fur inside the earflaps. He had pushed it back a little on his head, but otherwise made no accommodation to the heat. The woman behind the bar was smoking a cigarette on which nearly an inch of ash had accumulated. As I came in, she got rid of the ash by leaning forward in the direction of an ashtray on the bar and flicking the cigarette with her forefinger. The ash missed the ashtray by maybe three feet, and she absently brushed it off the bar and onto the floor.

I assumed she was a woman, because she wore a dress. But that was the only clue. Her graying hair looked as if it had been cut with a hatchet. She had a lipless slash of a mouth that went straight across her wide square face. Her eyebrows were thick and grew together over her nose, and her skin was gray and harsh. She stood with her massive forearms folded over her shapeless chest and raised her chin maybe an eighth of an inch in my direction. I glanced at my watch. It was quarter of ten in the morning.

"You got any coffee?" I said.

She shook her head.

One of the guys at the table said, "Hey, Gert, couple more."

She went around the bar and got their glasses. She took a couple of ice cubes out of a bag in the freezer top of the refrigerator, plunked one cube in each glass, poured some bourbon over it, and added ginger ale from a screw-top bottle. She walked back around, put the drinks down and said, "Two bucks."

Each of the drinkers gave her a dollar bill. She came back around the bar, put the two bills into a small, square, green metal box on the shelf. Then she looked at me again.

"Beer or hard stuff," she said. Her voice had a thick wheezy sound to it.

"Anything to eat?" I said.

"Got a Slim Jim," she said.

I shook my head. "I'm looking for a guy named Wilfred Pomeroy," I said.

She had no reaction. She didn't care if I was looking for Wilfred Pomeroy or not.

"Know him?" I said.

"Yuh."

"Know where I can find him?"

"Yuh."

"Where?"

She simply shook her head.

"Owe him money," I said. "I'm looking to pay him."

She looked across at the two fat guys drinking bourbon and ginger ale. Both of them wore high-laced leather boots. The steel toe of one showed through where the pale leather had worn away.

"Guy here says he owes Wilfred Pomeroy money," she said. The wheeze rattled in her chest. Her cigarette had burned down close to her lips. She spat it on the floor and let it smolder there while she got another one out of the pocket of her shapeless cotton dress. She lit it.

The guy in the "Day-Glo" cap said, "Shit."

Nobody else said anything.

"You're not buying that?" I said.

The other guy at the table said, "Wilfred never done nothing that anyone would owe him money for, mister."

The guy in the "Day-Glo" cap spat against the stove. It sizzled for a minute and then everything was quiet again.

"You from Boston or New York?" the other guy said.

"Boston," I said.

"How much that fancy jacket cost you?" "Day-Glo" said. At 9:50 in the morning he was already a little glassy-eyed. I was wearing jeans and a leather jacket, and in Tunnys Grill I felt like Little Lord Fauntleroy.

"Free," I said. "I took it away from a loudmouth in a barroom."

"Day-Glo's" brow furrowed for a minute while he thought about that.

"You think you're funny?" he said.

"No," I said, "I think you're funny. You know where I can find Wilfred Pomeroy, or not?"

"Maybe you want to get your wise city-boy ass stomped."

"Don't be a dope," I said. "You're half gassed already and you're fifty pounds out of shape."

"Day-Glo" looked at his pal.

"You want to show this city mister something?"

His pal was looking at me thoughtfully, or what passed for thoughtfully in Waymark. Then he made a dismissive gesture with his left hand.

"Fuck him, Francis."

The woman at the bar said, "You gonna buy something or not? If you ain't I don't want you loitering around my bar."

I looked around at the three of them, slowly.

"Have a nice day," I said, and departed haughtily. Mr. Charm, smooth-talking the bumpkins.

17

THE Waymark Town Hall was one of those Greek Revival buildings with white-pillared fronts that abound in the Berkshires. It stood at the end of a small wedge-shaped town common in its elegant white simplicity, like a fashion model at a rescue mission. Around back the land dropped off a level and the police and fire departments were housed there in the basement. The fire department was probably all volunteer. There were two engines and no people in the firehouse. Next to it was a single door in the concrete foundation wall, with a blue light beside it. I parked next to one of the gaudiest police cruisers ever customized. It had a light rack with two blue lights and a chrome siren mounted on the roof. There were chrome spotlights on both front window columns, running lights mounted on the fenders, and mud flaps and three antennas, and a giant shield painted on each door and on the hood in gold. Each one carried the legend WAYMARK POLICE. There was a shotgun locked upright at the dashboard, and a long black five-cell flashlight clipped beside it. The cruiser was painted light blue and white.

Inside the station was a square cinder-block room painted light green with a single large desk in front and a barred cell with wash basin, toilet and steel cot, in back. The cell door was ajar. There was a stuffed bobcat mounted on a slab of pine, sitting on top of a single file cabinet, there was a calendar on the wall with a picture of a stag at bay on it, and behind the desk sat a guy in a pale blue uniform shirt with white epaulets. A Sam Brown belt crossed over his chest, and a Western-style campaign hat sat on the desk in front of him next to the phone. A sign on the desk said BUFORD F. PHILLIPS, CHIEF. He had a big gold shield pinned to his chest. It too said CHIEF on it.

I took out my wallet and showed the chief my I.D.

I said, "I'm investigating a murder in Boston."

Phillips leaned back in his swivel chair and I could see the big pearl-handled .44 revolver he carried on the Sam Brown belt. He propped one foot up on an open drawer and held my wallet out a little to read it. He was wearing tooled leather cowboy boots.

"What the hell is this?" he said, studying my license at arm's length.

"Private detective," I said.

He didn't speak. He turned the wallet a little to catch the light better and compared my photo on the gun permit with the real me. While he was doing that, the tip of his tongue appeared between his lips, and his forehead wrinkled slightly. Studying things was hard work for Buford Phillips.

I waited. The room was quiet except for the sound of Phillips' breath coming noisily through his nose. He was very pale, the color of salt pork. His light hair was brush cut, and he was fat, the kind of puffed fat that seemed boneless, like an unbaked dinner roll.

Finally he slid my wallet back toward me.

"You carrying a gun?" he said.

I opened my jacket and showed him the gun.

"You got a license for that?"

"You just looked at it," I said.

He didn't have any reaction, just looked at me, and again, the tip of his tongue showed near the middle of his mouth.

"I'm looking for a guy named Wilfred Pomeroy," I said.

Phillips nodded.

"I'd like to question him about a murder in Boston."

Phillips nodded again.

"Would you know where he is?" I said.

"Who wants to know?" Phillips said.

I looked carefully around the office.

"Which of the people here," I said, "would you guess?"

"Hey, I asked you a question," Phillips said.

I took in a long breath.

"I would like to know where Wilfred Pomeroy is, so I may go and ask him some questions about a murder that took place recently in the city of Boston." I spoke very slowly.

Phillips nodded again.

"Where can I find him?" I said.

"Who was murdered?" Phillips said.

"Woman named Babe Loftus," I said.

"Sex murder?"

"No."

Phillips was silent again. His tongue moved about on his lip. His forehead wrinkled again.

"You think Wilfred did it?" he said.

"Don't know who did it," I said. "I'd just like to talk with him."

"If you don't know, why do you think it's Wilfred?"

I put my palms flat on Phillips' desk top and leaned over it until I was about six inches away from him and stared into his eyes.

"What the hell you doing?" Phillips said.

"Looking to see if there's anyone in there," I said.

"Hey, you got no business being a wise guy," Phillips said. "I got a right to make sure you're on the level."

"You sure yet?" I said.

"Yeah, yeah, you seem okay to me."

I straightened up. "Good," I said. "Can we go see Wilfred Pomeroy?"

"Sure, yeah, we can. I'll go with you. It's my town, you know, I got to make sure everything is done right, you know. It's my town."

"Dandy," I said. "Where's Wilfred?"

"I'll go along," Phillips said. "Take you there."

He let his chair come forward, and using the movement as propulsion he came to his feet. He shook his pants down over the tops of his boots; they were two inches too short and the boots looked too big, like the feet of a cartoon character. As Phillips came around the desk I noticed he had a blackjack in a low pocket on his striped uniform pants, and a come-along in a black leather case on his cartridge-studded belt. He got a pale blue jacket off a hook on the wall and slipped into it. The jacket had a mouton collar dyed a darker blue. He put on his campaign hat and waddled over to the door. He held it open, I went out, and he came after me and locked it.

"We'll go in the cruiser," he said.

I went around and waited until he got in and unlocked my side. Then I got in with him.

The cruiser fishtailed slightly on the snowy parking area as Phillips floored it in first, and we half skidded onto the plowed street, where the spinning rear wheels grabbed the dry pavement and sent the car squealing off west along the main street.

"An LTD," Phillips said. "Biggest engine they make."

I fumbled the safety belt around me and got it fastened.

"No use running," I said, "with you at the wheel."

"You can say that again, mister. You'd have to have a Corvette or something to get away from me."

We careened around a corner and up a short hill. The pavement stopped about twenty yards up the hill and the road became two ruts worn by oversized tires. The cruiser lurched and slithered as it went too fast for the road. There were trees on either side and a shambled stone wall on my side that slouched in disarray along the margin of the road among the leafless trees. Birches mostly, with an occasional maple.

In a clearing, where the road ended in a rutted turnaround, there was what appeared to be an old school bus with a shack built off of it. The shack was made of plywood and covered with felt paper. The paper had been nailed on with roofing nails, and their silver galvanized heads spotted randomly over the black surface. Tears in the paper had been repaired by nailing scraps of felt over the tear with more roofing nails, so that the studded appearance was without order. A stovepipe protruded through the roof of the shack, and a rusting fifty-gallon barrel stood on its side on two sawhorses next to the shack. I could smell kerosene. A big television antenna was nailed high in a tree above the shack and a cable ran from it into the shack. A power line snaked among the trees and ran down a weathered board into the shack. The windows of the bus were hung with cloth that looked mostly like it was made from potato sacks. Three mongrel dogs, all with their tails arching up over their hindquarters, came toward the cruiser, barking without rancor.

"This is Wilfred's place," Phillips said. "He done it himself."

"Handy," I said.

We walked across the snow-trampled, mud-mixed front lawn with the dogs roiling in a friendly fashion around our ankles. They were all about 35 pounds, tan blending to black. They were of parentage so mixed that they had regressed to basic Dog, nearly identical with mongrel dogs in China and Bolivia.

Phillips banged on the door.

"Hey, Wilfred," he yelled, "it's Chief Phillips."

The door opened slowly and stopped halfway.

"What do you want?" someone said.

Phillips shoved the door fully open.

"Come on, come on, Wilfred. This is official business."

Phillips walked through the fully open door, and I followed him.

Pomeroy was a sturdily built, middle-sized guy with a big guardsman mustache, and brown curly hair that fell in a kind of love curl over his forehead. He was wearing jeans and a maroon sweatshirt with a hood. UMASS was printed across the front of the sweatshirt, in big letters. The first thing that I noticed about the shack was that it was neat. The second thing I noticed was the huge poster of Jill Joyce that nearly filled the wall above the bed. It was a publicity poster for a previous show, and it showed Jill in a frilly apron looking delectably confused over a steamy pot.

"Wilfred," Phillips said, "this here is a guy named Spenser. He's a detective, from Boston, and he wants to talk to you about some murder."

"I love your technique, Chief," I said. "First put him at ease."

"I don't know about no murder," Pomeroy said.

I put my hand out.

Pomeroy took it without enthusiasm. He had one

of those handshakes that die on contact. It was like shaking hands with a noodle. The three dogs had come in with us and repaired to various places of repose; one, presumably the alpha dog, was curled on the bed. The other two lay on the floor near the kerosene stove. Everything in the place was folded neatly, secured just right, dusted and aligned. The bed was covered with an Army blanket with hospital corners. Everywhere on the walls were pictures, mostly clipped from magazines, tacked to the exposed two-by-fours that framed the shack. The walls themselves were simply the uncovered kraft paper backing of fiberglass insulation. There were pictures of movie stars, of singers and television performers, famous politicians, athletes, writers, scientists, and business tycoons. There was a picture of Lee Iacocca clipped from a magazine cover, and one of Norman Mailer. I saw no famous detectives.

Pomeroy's table was an upended cable spool with oilcloth tacked to the top. The oilcloth was a red-checkered pattern and shone as if it had just been washed. Pomeroy moved behind the table.

"What do you want?" he said again. His eyes were big and soft and eager for approval.

"Just some questions," I said. The kerosene stove was pouring out heat. "Mind if I take off my jacket?"

He shook his head. I took off my leather jacket and hung it on a hook on the back of the door where his red plaid mackinaw hung. He looked at the gun under my arm without saying anything. Phillips went and pushed the dog out of the way and sat on the bed. He left his coat on. The dog gave a short sigh and moved to the foot of the bed and turned around twice and lay down again.

"Nice poster of Jill Joyce," I said. "She your favorite?"

He nodded.

"You know she's in Boston now shooting her series."

He nodded again.

"She didn't get killed," he said. "I'd a seen it on TV if she got killed."

"No," I said, "she's fine."

"You know her?" Pomeroy said.

"Yes," I said.

We were quiet. One of the dogs sleeping by the stove got up and went over and sniffed at Phillips' shoe. Phillips pushed it away with his foot. I saw Pomeroy's eyes shift nervously.

"Don't be rude to the dog," I said to Phillips. "Dog lives here and you don't."

Phillips got two bright spots on his pale cheeks.

"Who the hell you talking to?" he said. His hand brushed instinctively against his gun butt. I turned my head slowly and looked at him without saying anything.

"I don't like dogs," he said.

I looked at him for another moment, then turned back to Pomeroy.

"Do you know her?" I said.

"Jill?"

"Yeah."

He shook his head slowly. "No. I'm a big fan of hers, but I don't know her."

"I heard you did know her," I said.

Pomeroy looked past me nervously.

"No, honest."

"I heard you knew her pretty well," I said. "Guy named Randall says you knew her."

The big soft eyes got wider and less focused. His gaze moved around the room, looking for someplace to settle.

"I haven't been near her since he said."

"How'd you get to know her in the first place?" I said.

Pomeroy shook his head.

"Why not?" I said. "What's not to talk about?"

Pomeroy looked at Phillips. I nodded, lifted my jacket off the back of the door and shrugged it on, lifted his off and handed it to him.

"You cover it here," I said to Phillips. "Wilfred and I will take a walk."

"You need me to back you up?" Phillips said.

"No, I'll be okay," I said.

When the dogs saw Pomeroy put his jacket on, all three of them were at the door, mouths open, tongues lolling, tails wagging. I opened the door and they surged out ahead of us and stopped in the yard looking back.

"Come on," I said.

Pomeroy went past me and I followed him and shut the door. The dogs moved out ahead of us in a businesslike way, sniffing along sinuous spoors, wagging their tails. The woods were empty at this time of year except for squirrels. The midday sun was warm in the southern sky and water dripped from the tree branches and made half-dollar-sized holes around the trees in the crust of the old snow. We followed the dogs along a path among the trees that had been pressed out by footfalls.

"Phillips is a mean bastard," Pomeroy said. He never looked at me as he spoke, and his speech was soft.

I nodded. Pomeroy seemed to sense my agreement even though he didn't appear to be looking at me.

"These dogs are like my family," he said.

"Yeah," I said.

"I don't have anything else," he said.

"Yeah."

There seemed no purpose to the path we were on. It meandered through the second-growth forest. Under the evergreens, where the snow was thin, dark pine needles and matted leaves were slick with ice and snow melt. The dogs ranged ahead of us, sniffing intently at the ground, and swinging back in singly or together to look at us before they ranged away again. We came up a low rise and looked down into a shallow swale where ground-water stood, frozen and snow covered. The flat surface was crisscrossed with dog tracks, and among them, bird tracks, partridge maybe, or pheasant.

We stopped and looked down at the swale. The trees and brush grew thickly right to its banks.

"I was married to her once," Pomeroy said.

He was staring down into the swale. I didn't say anything. It was as if he were a shattered cup, badly mended, with the shards of himself barely clinging together. I stayed very still. One of the dogs came back from ranging and sat on Pomeroy's feet and looked down at the swale too.

"You don't believe me," he said.

"Yes," I said, "I do."

"I used to tell people, but they never believed me. Most people think I'm a little off anyway."

He reached a hand down absently toward the dog. The dog lapped it industriously.

"I probably am a little off," he said.

"Maybe nobody's on," I said. "Maybe there's nothing to be off of."

He glanced at me for a moment. I nearly lost him. Then he shook his head and shrugged. Spenser the philosopher king.

"Guy lives in the woods with three dogs," he said. "Guy like that isn't all with it, you know?"

"When were you married?" I said.

He paused a moment, a little startled, trying to remember what he'd been saying about marriage.

"Nineteen sixty-eight," he said. "I was in the Navy in San Diego, I met her in a bar."

"Love at first sight?"

"For me."

"How about her?"

"She was seventeen. She liked the uniform, maybe."

The other two dogs came out of the woods and circled along the rim of the swale and sat down near us, their tongues out, and looked at us.

"How long did it last?" I said.

"She ran away in a month. I never saw her again."

"Until?"

"Until she came to Boston."

"So you did try to see her," I said.

He didn't answer. The dog at his feet rose suddenly and made off with its nose to the ground. The two others followed. They went over the hill on the far side and out of sight and in a minute we could hear them yelping.

"Rabbit," Pomeroy said.

I waited. The yelping faded, then stopped.

"I wanted to see her. After all that time, I . . . the month I was with her was . . ." He shrugged, spread his hands. "It was my best month," he said.

The dogs trotted back, single file, and sat and looked at us again.

"She wasn't friendly," I said.

"No. She . . . what the hell. She's a big star and I'm . . . look at me, you know?"

I nodded.

"But you persisted."

"Persisted," he said, rolling the word around like a piece of strange candy. "I wanted to see her," he said finally. "I'm not much, but I am married to her."

"Still?" I said.

"I never divorced her. I never heard from her. Far as I know we're still married."

"Was Jill Joyce her name then?"

"No." For the first time since I'd met him Pomeroy almost smiled. "It was Jillian Zabriskie."

"She born in San Diego?"

He nodded. "I never met her parents," he said, "but I'm pretty sure they were around there somewhere."

"Why'd she run off?"

"She never said. One day I came home and she wasn't there and she was never there again."

"You look for her?"

"Sure. I told the police and stuff. Everyone who knew anything about her knew she was wild. Everyone assumed she run off with somebody."

"You think so?"

"She always liked men," he said.

"What was the name of the bar?" I said.

"Pancho Doyle's," he said. I knew he'd remember.

"Still there?" I said.

"I don't know. After I got discharged I never went back to San Diego. I just come home here. I was a radar man when I got out. I went to Worcester Tech for a semester, gonna be an engineer, but . . ." He shrugged.

"Honorable discharge?" I said.

"They kicked me out," he said. "I was drinking."

"Worcester Tech?"

He nodded. "I was drinking more. I dropped out."

"Still drink?" I said.

He shook his head. "AA," he said. "Been sober five years in March."

"So you called Jill Joyce and she told you to take a hike, and you kept calling and finally a guy named Randall came to see you."

"He was very scary," Pomeroy said. He was staring down at the ground in front of him.

"What'd he say?"

"He shoved me around a little, and he said I was to stay away from Jill Joyce or I'd be sorry. He was kicking my dogs too."

"For what it's worth," I said, "I kicked him in the balls a few days ago."

Pomeroy looked up at me, a little startled. "You did?"

"Thought you might like to know that."

"I would. Ah, you . . . you must be pretty tough."

"I think so," I said. "You ever threaten Jill Joyce?"

"Me? No. I couldn't . . ."

"You know anyone named Babe Loftus?"

He shook his head.

"You work?" I said.

"A little, lawns in the summer. Shovel some sidewalks. Mostly I get welfare."

"Anything from Jill?"

He shook his head.

"You got any idea why anyone would threaten Jill Joyce, want to kill her?"

"Somebody tried to kill her?"

"Somebody killed her stunt double. Whether it was a mistake or a warning, none of us know."

"I wouldn't want her to get hurt," Pomeroy said.

"Lot of people would, I think. I don't know what

she was in San Diego twenty-five years ago, but she's turned into a high-octane pain in the ass since."

Pomeroy didn't say anything. We turned away from the swale and walked back through the woods, the dogs coursing ahead of us, one or another of them looking back over its shoulder now and then to be sure we were there.

"Took your damned sweet time," Phillips said when we got there.

"Boy, that police training," I said. "You don't miss a trick."

18

HAWK sat in perfect repose on the wide window sill in Salzman's office, with the winter landscape behind him. He had on a white shirt and black jeans and black cowboy boots and a black leather shoulder holster containing a pearl-handled, chrome-plated .44 mag, excellent against low-flying aircraft. Salzman was at his desk. Jill was on the couch, her legs tucked demurely under her, a bright plaid skirt tucked around her knees. I was pacing.

"You tell me you don't know Rojack," I said. "I go out there and find out you do. You tell me you never heard of Wilfred Pomeroy. I go out there and he tells me you're married."

"He's a liar," Jill said serenely. "I never have heard of him."

"He tells me that you never got a divorce."

"I did too," Jill said. "I told you he's a liar."

Hawk smiled from the window sill, like a man appreciating a funny remark.

"If you had told me the truth you'd have saved me a couple of days' driving and talking."

"Sandy," Jill said, "are you going to let him treat me this way?"

"He's trying to help you, Jilly, like we all are."

"The hell he is," Jill said. "He's trying to dig up a lot of dirt from my past and make something out of it."

"Like sense," I said.

"I wouldn't be surprised if he was really working for one of those shows," she said. She glanced at Hawk.

"Geraldo Spenser," Hawk said.

"Don't be fooled," I said, "by my good looks. I'm just a simple gumshoe."

"Simple snoop," Jill said. She was warming to her role. She'd decided her motivation and had a real handle on her character. "I hired you to protect me, not to snoop around looking for cruddy gossip."

"That's a tautology," I said.

"Whaat?" Jill said. She cocked her head a little and her eyelashes nearly fluttered. Cute was what she did when she didn't understand something.

"All gossip is cruddy," Hawk said.

"I don't care," Jill said. "I don't want him around; get rid of him. Hawk will protect me."

"Nope," Hawk said.

Jill's head swiveled toward him and there was real alarm in her face.

"No?"

"I work for him." Hawk nodded toward me. "He go, I go."

"You work for me," Jill said.

Hawk smiled pleasantly and shook his head. Jill looked back at me and then to Hawk.

"You don't mean that, Hawk," she said. She

moved her body a little on the couch and waited for Hawk to bark. He didn't.

"Jill . . ." Sandy said.

"You fucking men." Jill's face was red. "You're good for one thing. All I deal with is men, I got no one to trust, no one to talk to, no one who gives a shit about me." Tears started down her face. "I want them gone, off this set, out of here. Now. Goddamned . . ."

Salzman got up and walked around his desk. "Jilly," he said and put an arm around her shoulder. "Jilly, come on. We'll work this out. You work so hard, you're tired." He patted her shoulder. She leaned her head against his hip. "Jilly, take a break. Here, I'll get Molly to walk over to your trailer with you. Come on."

He eased Jill to her feet and with an arm around her edged her to the door.

"Oh, Sandy," Jill was sniffling. "Oh, Sandy, sometimes I feel so alone."

"You're a star, honey. It happens to stars. But I'm here for you, all of us are."

"Not those two bastards," Jill said.

"Sure. I'll straighten that out, Jilly," Salzman said. He sounded like he was talking to an excitable puppy.

They walked that way to the door. Salzman opened it.

"Molly," he said to a woman at the desk in the outer office. "Take Jill to her trailer and stay with her. She's not feeling well."

"Sure, Sandy."

Molly put her arm through Jill's and squeezed it.

"Got some coffee over there, Jill?" Molly said. "Maybe get some cake. Some girl talk? Who needs men."

Jill went with her. As they left, Molly, who was dark-eyed and thin-faced, gave Salzman a look of savage reproach over her shoulder. Salzman shrugged and came back into his office and closed the door. He rubbed his hands over his face.

"Christ," he said.

He stood that way for a moment, rubbing his face, then he turned and went back behind his desk. He looked at me and Hawk.

"How are we going to work this?" he said.

"Can you stand her?" I said to Hawk.

"Seen worse," Hawk said.

"Jesus," Salzman said. "I'd like to know where."

I said, "So we'll keep Hawk with her, and I'll try to run this thing down. You can tell her you fired me and prevailed upon my, ah, colleague to stay on."

"What are you going to do?" Salzman said.

"I've got another name. I'll go see if I can find the name and ask some questions and get other names and go see them and ask them questions and . . ." I spread my hands.

"Magic," Hawk said.

"What's this gonna cost me?" Salzman said.

"A round trip to San Diego," I said.

"Can't you call?" Salzman said.

"Yeah, but it's not the same. You don't see people,

you don't notice peripheral things, people don't see you."

"Why should they see you?" Salzman said.

"Case you big and mean-looking like him," Hawk said, "might be able to scare them a little."

"Ahhh," Salzman said. "Okay, probably cheaper than Jill's bar bill, anyway."

19

THE slender mirrored face of the John Hancock Building rose fifty stories on the southern edge of Copley Square, reflecting the big brownstone Trinity Church back upon itself. Across the new plaza, snow covered now and crisscrossed with footpaths, opposite the church was the Public Library. There were Christmas lights in the square, and the uniformed doorman at the Copley Plaza stood between the gilded lions and whistled piercingly for a cab. I'd always wanted to do that and never been able to. *Anyone can whistle, any old time, easy.* I pursed my lips and whistled quietly. I put two fingers in my mouth and blew. There was a flat-sounding rush of air. *So what?* I headed for the library with the doorman's whistle soaring across Dartmouth Street. *The hell with whistling.* I went past the bums lounging in the weak winter sun on the wide steps to the old entrance, and went in the ugly new entrance on Boylston Street.

A half hour among the out-of-town phone directories gave me three Zabriskies in greater San Diego. I copied down addresses and phone numbers, and walked back down Boylston Street toward my office.

When I went inside, Martin Quirk was sitting at my desk with his feet up.

"Spenser," I said. "Boy, you're much uglier than I'd heard."

Quirk let his feet down and stood and walked around to the chair in front of my desk, the one for clients, when any came to my office.

"You don't get any funnier," Quirk said.

"But I don't get discouraged, either," I said.

"Too bad," Quirk said.

I sat behind my desk. He sat in the client chair.

I said, "Can you whistle, loud, like doormen do?"

"No."

"Me either. You ever wonder why that is?"

"No."

"No, I suppose you wouldn't," I said.

I swiveled half around in my chair and pulled out a bottom drawer and put my right foot on it. I could see out the window that way, down to the corner where Berkeley crosses Boylston. There were people out in large number, carrying packages. I looked back at Quirk. He always looked the same. Short black hair, tweed jacket, dark knit tie, white shirt with a pronounced roll in the button-down collar. His hands were pale and strong-looking with long blunt fingers and black hair on the backs. Everything fit, and since Quirk was about my size, it meant he shopped the Big Man stores or had the clothes made. He'd been the homicide commander for a long time, and he probably should have been police commissioner except that nothing intimidated him, and he wasn't careful what he said.

"What you got on this TV killing?" he said.

"Babe Loftus?"

"Un huh."

"Nothing directly. Jill is not an open book," I said. "She sort of doesn't get it that I'm working for her."

"She doesn't get that about us, either."

"What have you got?" I said.

"I asked you first," Quirk said.

"I know she's had a relationship with a guy named Rojack, lives out in Dover."

"Stanley," Quirk said. "Got a big geek of a bodyguard named Randall."

"Yes," I said.

"Whom you knocked on his ass in front of the Charles one morning last week."

"It seemed the right thing to do," I said.

"It was," Quirk said.

"Jill's story is she doesn't know him, and anyway he's a creep."

"Tell me about him," Quirk said. "What you know."

I did, everything except the detail about Wilfred Pomeroy.

"Don't underestimate Randall," Quirk said when I finished. "He's bad news."

"Me too," I said.

Quirk nodded, a little tiredly. "Yeah," he said. "Aren't we all." He scrubbed along his jawline with the palms of both hands. Across Boylston Street there were three or four guys in coveralls stringing Christmas lights around Louis'.

"Rojack is not exactly a wise guy," Quirk said, "and he's not exactly Chamber of Commerce. He's a developer and what he develops is money. He's enough on the wild side to have a bodyguard. He gets to go to receptions at City Hall, and I'm sure he's got Joe Broz's unlisted number."

I nodded.

"You want something fixed, he's a good guy to see. People he does business with are shooters, but Rojack stays out in Dover and has lunch at Locke's."

"He's dirty," I said.

"Yeah, he's dirty; but almost always it's secondhand, under the table, behind the back. We usually bust somebody else and Rojack goes home to Dover."

"Why would he shoot Babe Loftus?" I said.

Quirk shrugged.

"What's the autopsy say?"

"Shot once, at close range, in the back, with a three fifty-seven magnum, bullet entered her back below the left shoulder blade at an angle, penetrated her heart and lodged under her right rib cage. She was dead probably before she felt anything."

"Think the killer's left-handed?" I said.

"If he stood directly behind her," Quirk said, "which he may or may not have done. Even if he is, it narrows the suspects down to maybe, what, five hundred thousand in the Commonwealth?"

"Or maybe he was right-handed and shot her that way so you'd think he was left-handed."

"Or maybe he was ambidextrous, and a midget, and he stood on a box," Quirk said. "You been reading Philo Vance again?"

"So young," I said, "yet so cynical."

"What else you got?" Quirk said.

"That's it," I said.

"You think it's mistaken identity?"

"I don't know."

"You think Rojack did it, or had Randall do it?"

"No."

"Why not?" Quirk said.

"Doesn't seem his style," I said.

Outside the light was gone. The early winter evening had settled and the artificial light in storefronts and on street corners had taken hold. Nothing like colored light to spruce up a city.

"Why do I think you know more than you're telling?" Quirk said.

"Because you've been a copper too long. It's made you suspicious and skeptical."

"I've known you too long," Quirk said.

I was about to make a devastating response when my door opened and Susan came in, bringing with her a light scent of lilac. Quirk rose and Susan came and kissed him on the cheek.

"If you are going to arrest him, Martin, could you wait until he's taken me to dinner?"

"If being a pain in the ass were illegal," Quirk said, "he'd be doing life in Walpole."

"He's kind of cute, though, don't you think?"

"Cuter than lace pants," Quirk said.

20

It was one of my favorite times in winter, the part of the day when it is dark, but the offices haven't let out yet. All the windows are still lighted, and people are at their desks and walking about in the offices—bright vignettes of ordinary life.

Susan and I held hands as we strolled down Boylston Street toward Arlington. The store windows were full of red bows, and Santa cut-outs, and tinsel rope, and fake snow. Real snow had begun again, lightly, in big flakes that meandered down. Not the kind of snow that would pile up. Just the kind of snow the Chamber of Commerce would have ordered pre-Christmas. After the recent chill it was mild by comparison, maybe thirty degrees. Susan was wearing a black hip-length leather coat with fake black fur on the collar. Her head was bare and she wore her thick black hair up today. A few of the snowflakes settled on it.

"No fur coat?"

"Last time I wore it someone in Harvard Square called me a murderer."

"That's because they haven't met a real murderer," I said.

"Still, I don't feel right wearing it," Susan said. "The animals do suffer."

"You didn't know that?" I said.

"No. I had this lovely little vision of them romping about in green pastures until they died a quiet death of natural causes."

"Of course," I said. "Who would think otherwise?"

"I know, it's a ludicrous idea; but when they said ranch raised that's what I thought."

"Complicity's hard to avoid," I said.

"Probably impossible," Susan said. "But it doesn't hurt to try a little."

"Especially when it's easy," I said.

"Like giving up fur," Susan said. She banged her head gently against my shoulder. "Next I may have to reexamine my stand on whales."

The snow was falling fast enough now to give the illusion of snowfall, without any real threat of a blizzard. The stoplights fuzzed a little in the falling snow, radiating red or green in a kind of impressionist splash in the night. We turned left on Arlington and walked past the Ritz. Across the street, in the Public Garden, Washington sat astride his enormous horse, in oblivious dignity as the snow drifted down past him. To our left, the mall ran down Commonwealth Avenue. There was a man walking his dog on the mall. The dog was a pointer of some kind and kept shying against the man's knee as the snow fluttered about her. Every few steps she would look up at the man as if questioning the sense of a walk in these conditions.

The next block was mine, and we turned down Marlborough Street and into my apartment. Susan looked around as she took off her coat and draped it over the back of one of my counter stools.

"Well," she said, "fire laid already, table set for two. Wineglasses?"

She shook her hair a little to get rid of the snowflakes, her hand making those automatic female gestures which women make around their hair.

"What did you have in mind?" she said.

"I'd like to emulate the fire," I said. "Shall we start with a cocktail?"

"We'd be fools not to," Susan said.

"Okay," I said. "You light the fire while I mix them up."

"Jewish women don't make fires," Susan said.

"It's all made," I said. "Just light the paper in three or four places."

"All right," she said, "I'll try. But I don't want to get any icky soot on me."

She crouched in front of the fire, smoothing her skirt under her thighs as she did so, and struck a match. I went around the counter into my kitchen and made vodka martinis. I stirred them in the pitcher with a long spoon. I used to stir them with the blade of a kitchen knife until Susan saw me do it one day and went immediately out to buy me a long-handled silver spoon. I put Susan's in a stemmed martini glass with four olives and no ice.

I put mine in a thick lowball glass over ice with a twist. I put both drinks on a little lacquer tray and brought them around and put them on the coffee table.

The fire was going and the paper had already ignited the kindling. Small ventures of flame danced around the edge of the yet unburning logs. Susan had retired to the couch, her feet tucked up under her. She had on a black skirt and a crimson blouse, open at the throat with a gold chain showing. Her earrings were gold teardrops. She had enormous dark eyes and a very wide mouth and her neck, where it showed at the open throat of the blouse, was strong.

Susan and I clinked glasses and drank.

"That's a very good martini," Susan said.

"Spenser," I said, "the martini king."

"What time do you leave tomorrow?" Susan said.

"Nine A.M.," I said. "American flight 11. First class."

"You deserve no less," Susan said.

"Mindy," I said, "the production coordinator. She looked at me and said clearly I don't fit well in coach. She said everyone else travels first class at Zenith Meridien."

"Nonstop?" Susan said.

"To L.A.," I said. "I'll drive down from there. Nothing nonstop from Boston to San Diego."

"I'll miss you," Susan said.

"Yes," I said. "I don't like to leave you."

The logs had begun to catch in the fireplace, and

the fire got deeper and richer and both of us stared into it in silence.

"You ever wonder why people stare into fires?" I said.

"Yes," Susan said. She had shifted on the couch and now sat with her head on my shoulder. She held her martini in both hands and drank it in very sparing sips.

"You ever figure out why?"

"No."

"You're a shrink," I said. "You're supposed to know stuff like that."

"Oh," Susan said. "That's right. Well, it's probably a somatic impulse rooted in neonatal adaptivity. People will gaze at clothes in a dryer, too."

"I liked your previous answer better," I said.

"Me too," Susan said.

We looked at the fire some more. As the logs became fully involved in the fire they settled in upon each other and burned stronger. Susan finished her martini.

"What's for chow?" she said.

"Duck breast sliced on the diagonal and served rare, onion marmalade, brown rice, broccoli tossed with a spoonful of sesame tahini."

"Sounds toothsome," Susan said.

"You have several options in relationship to dinner and other matters," I said.

"Un huh?"

"You may make love with me before or after dinner," I said. "That's one option."

"Un huh."

"You may make love with me here on the couch, or you and I may retire to the bedroom."

"Un huh."

"You make take the time to disrobe, or you may enjoy me in whatever disarray we create with our spontaneity."

Susan ticked off the various choices thoughtfully on the fingers of her left hand.

"Are there any other choices?" she said.

"You may shower if you wish," I said.

Susan turned her face toward me with that look of adult play in her eyes that I'd never seen anyone emulate.

"I showered before I came to your office," she said.

"Am I to take that to imply that you intended to, ah, boff me even before you arrived?"

"You're the detective," Susan said. "You figure it out. I opt for now, here, in disarray."

And she put her arms around my neck and pressed her mouth against mine.

"Good choice," I murmured.

21

THE drive down the San Diego Freeway from LAX takes about two and a half hours and seems like a week. Once you get below the reaches of L.A.'s industrial sprawl, the landscape is sere and unfriendly. The names of the beach towns come up and flash past and recede: Huntington Beach, Newport Beach, Laguna, San Clemente. But you can't see them from the freeway. Just the signs and the roads curving off through the brownish hills.

Mindy had gotten me a hotel room at the Hyatt Islandia in Mission Bay, and I pulled in there around 3:30 in the afternoon with the temperature at eighty-six and the sky cloudless. They assigned me a room in one of the pseudo-rustic cabanas that ran along the bay, as a kind of meandering wing to the tall central hotel building. I stashed my bag, got my list of addresses and my city map, and headed back out to work.

San Diego, like San Francisco, and like Seattle, seems defined by its embrace of the sea. The presence of the Pacific Ocean is assertive even when the ocean itself is out of sight. There is a different ambient brightness where the steady sunshine hits the water and diffuses. The bay, the Navy, the bridge to

Coronado seemed always there, even when you couldn't see them.

Of my three Zabriskies, two lived downtown; the third was up the coast a little in Esmeralda. The first one was a Chief Petty Officer who was at sea on a carrier. His wife said he didn't have any sisters, that his mother was in Aiken, South Carolina, and that she herself never watched television. The second was a Polish émigré who had arrived from Gdansk fourteen months ago. It took me into the evening to find that out. I had supper in a place near the hotel, on the bay, that advertised fresh salmon broiled over alder logs. I went in and ate some with a couple of bottles of Corona beer (hold the lime). It wasn't as good as I had hoped it would be; it still tasted like fish. After supper I strolled back to the hotel along the bayfront, past the charter boat shanties and the seafood take-out stands that sold ice and soda. Across the expressway, gleaming with light in the murmuring subtropical evening, the tower of Sea World rose above the lowland where the bay had been created. It was maybe 9:30 on the coast, and half past midnight on my eastern time sensor. Susan would be asleep at home, the snow drifting harmlessly outside her window. She would sleep nearly motionless, waking in the same position as she'd gone to sleep. She rarely moved in the night. Jill Joyce would have gone to sleep drunk, by now; and she would wake up clear-eyed and innocent-looking in the morning to go in front of the camera and charm the hearts of America. Babe Loftus wouldn't.

In my cabana I undressed and hung my clothes up carefully. There was nothing on the tube worth watching. I turned out the light and lay quietly, three thousand miles from home, and listened to the waters of the bay murmur across from my window, and smelled the water, a mild placid smell in the warm, faraway night.

22

ESMERALDA is in a canyon on the north edge of San Diego. It nestles against the Pacific Ocean with the hills rising behind it to cut off the rest of California as if it didn't exist. Esmeralda was full of trees and gardens and flowers. The downtown lounged along the coastline, a highlight of stucco and Spanish tile and plate glass and polished brass clustered near Esmeralda cove. One would never starve in Esmeralda. Every third building along the main drag was a restaurant. The other ones sold jewelry and antiques and designer fashions. The pink stucco hotel in the middle of the main drag had a big canopied patio out front and a discreet sign that said CASA DEL PONIENTE. Three valet carhops stood alertly outside in black vests and white shirts waiting to do anything you told them to do. I nosed in and parked in front of a bookstore across the street from the hotel. According to my map, Polton's Lane ran behind the stores that fronted Main Street. I left the car and walked back to the corner and turned left on Juniper Avenue. The street was lined with eucalyptus trees that sagged heavily, their branches nearly touching the ground in some places. There was a luggage shop, the window display a single suitcase with a fuchsia silk scarf draped over it. The suitcase and scarf sat on a black velvet background under a small spotlight. Beyond the luggage store was a discreet real estate office done in pale gray and plum, with color pictures, well mounted, of oceanfront property displayed in the window. Between the two buildings was Polton's Lane. The name was too grand. It was an alley. Behind the stores, cartons and trash barrels were piled, overflowing in some cases. Two cats, a yellow tom with tattered ears, and something that had once been mostly white, scuttled out of sight, their tails pointed straight out as they hurried away.

The alley widened into a small vacant lot encircled by the back doors of affluence. In the lot were several small frame shacks, probably one room apiece, with low board porches across the front. To each had been attached a lean-to which probably was a bathroom. The yard in front of the one nearest to me was bare dirt. The rest of the lot was weeds. The rusting hulk of a car that might once have been a Volvo stood doorless and wheelless among the weeds, and beyond it someone had discarded a hot water heater. A line of utility poles preceded me down the alley, and wires swung lax between the poles and each house. I stood staring at this odd community of hovels, built perhaps before the town had acquired a main street; built maybe by the workers who built the main street. Here and there among the weeds were automobile tires and beer cans, and at least one mattress with the stuffing spilled out.

My address was number three. Once, a long time

ago, someone had tried to make a front path of concrete squares set into the ground. Now they were barely visible among the weed overgrowth. From the house came the sound of a television set blaring a talk show. On the front porch a couple of green plastic bags had torn open, and the contents spilled out onto the porch floor. It didn't look as if it had happened recently. It was hot in the backside of Esmeralda, and in the heat the rank smell of the weeds mixed with whatever had rotted in the trash bags. I maneuvered around the trash and knocked on the screen door that hung loose in its hinges from a badly warped doorjamb. Nothing happened. I knocked again. Through the screen, which was, it seemed, the only door, I could see a steel-framed cot, with a mattress and a pink quilt and a pillow with no pillowcase. Next to it was a soapstone sink, and in front of both was a metal table that had once been coated with white enamel. To the right of the door I could see the back of what might have been a rocking chair. It moved a little and then a woman appeared in the doorway. The smell of booze came with her, overpowering the smell of the weeds and the hot barren earth.

"Yuh," she said.

She was an angular woman with white hair through which faded streaks of blond still showed. The hair hung straight down around her face without any hint of a comb. She had on a tee shirt that advertised beer, and a pair of miracle fiber slacks that had probably started out yellow. Her feet were bare.

In her right hand she was carrying a bottle of Southern Comfort, her skinny, blue-veined hand clamped around its neck.

"Spenser," I said. "City Services. Open up."

The door was hooked shut, although the screening in front of it was torn and I could have reached in and unhooked it myself.

She nodded slowly, staring at me through the door. Her face had not seen make-up, or sun, for a long time. It sagged along her jawline, and puckered at the corners of her mouth. Her eyes were darkly circled and pouchy. In the hand that didn't hold the Southern Comfort was a cigarette, and she brought it up slowly, as if trying to remember the way, and took a big suck on it.

"Vera Zabriskie?" I said. I made it sound officious and impatient. Women like Vera Zabriskie were used to civil servants snapping at them. It was what they endured in return for the welfare check that kept them alive. She looked at me, still frowning, as she let the smoke drift out of her mouth. Then she took a slug of Southern Comfort from the bottle and swallowed.

"Yuh," she said.

"You're Vera?" I said.

She nodded.

"Well, then, damn it, let me in. You think I got all day?"

She thought about what I'd said, turned it around a little in her head, got a look at it, and figured out, slowly, what it meant. Still holding the cigarette between the first two fingers, she raised a hand and fumbled the hook out of the door. She stepped back. I pushed it open and went in. The place smelled bad, a scent compounded of garbage, sweat, booze, cigarette smoke, and loss. A huge color television set was blatting at me from the corner. On top of the television set, framed in one of those cardboard holders that school pictures come in, was a color picture of Jill Joyce on the cover of *TV Guide.* The picture didn't fit the frame right, and it had been adjusted with Scotch tape here and there. *Can this be a clue I see before me?*

Vera Zabriskie went back to her rocking chair and sat in it and took a pull on the Southern Comfort bottle, and stared at the tube. It stared back with about the same level of comprehension. She dropped her burning cigarette on the floor and stamped aimlessly at it and half squashed it. The crushed butt continued to smolder. The floor around her chair was littered with sniped cigarettes and burn marks in the unfinished plywood.

I went around and turned off the television. She showed no reaction. She continued to look at the blank screen.

I said, "Who's the woman in the picture?"

Her head turned slowly toward me. She squinted a little. She raised her left hand and realized there was no cigarette and stopped, put the bottle of Southern Comfort on the floor, picked up a pack of Camels from the floor and got another cigarette burning. She inhaled deeply, put down the pack, picked up the jug, and stared at me again.

"Who's the woman in the picture?" I said.

"Jillian."

"Jillian who?" I said. I still had my official tone.

"Jillian Zabriskie," she said with no inflection. "I seen the name on a TV show."

"She related to you?"

"Daughter," she said. There was a sound in her voice that I hadn't heard before. It was weak but it might have been pride. I looked around the one-room shack where Vera Zabriskie lived. She saw me look around. I saw her see me. We stared for a moment at each other, like two actual humans. For a moment a real person lurked inside the mask of alcohol and defeat, and peered out at me through the rheumy blue eyes. For a moment I wasn't a guy pumping her for information.

"You're not close with your daughter," I said.

Vera suddenly heaved herself up out of the rocker. She put the cigarette in her mouth and put the bottle on the chipped enamel table. She opened the drawer in the table and rummaged with both hands, and came out with another picture.

It was framed in cardboard, like the picture of Jill, only this one was a school picture. Vera handed it to me. It was a picture of a little girl, maybe ten. Dark hair, dark eyes, olive skin, and a clear resemblance to Jill Joyce.

"Who's this?" I said.

"Granddaughter," she said.

"Jillian's daughter?" I said.

"Yuh."

I looked at the picture again. In the indefinable way that pictures speak, this one was telling me it wasn't recent.

"How old is she now?" I said.

"Jillian?"

"No, your granddaughter."

The burst of humanity had drained her. She was back in the rocker, with her bottle. She shrugged. Her gaze was fixed on the blank picture tube. I slipped the picture out of its holder and put it inside my shirt. Then I folded the cardboard and put it back in the drawer.

"You see her much?"

She shook her head.

"She live around here?"

She shook her head again. She drank a little Southern Comfort from the bottle.

"Far away?"

She nodded.

"Where?"

"L.A.," Vera said. Her voice was flatter than a tin shingle.

"She with her dad?" I said. *Sincere, interested in Vera's family. You're in good hands with Spenser.*

Vera shrugged.

"What's her dad's name?"

"Greaser," Vera said clearly.

"Odd name," I said.

"Told her stay away from that greaser. Took my granddaughter."

"What did you say his name was?"

"Spic name."

"Un huh," I said helpfully.

"Told her not."

"What's his name?" The helpful smile stretched across my face like oil on water. I could feel the tension behind my shoulders as I tried to squeeze blood from this stone.

"Victor," she said. "Victor del Rio."

"And he lives in L.A."

"Yuh."

"You know where?"

She shook her head.

"You ever see your granddaughter?"

She shook her head again. She was frowning at the blank television, as if the fact of its gray silence had just begun to penetrate. She leaned forward in the rocker and turned it on. Then, exhausted by the effort of concentration, she leaned back in the rocker and took a long pull of her Southern Comfort. The talk show had given way to a game show; photogenic contestants frantic to win the money, a faintly patronizing host, amused by their greed.

I stood silently beside the seated woman lost in her television and her booze. She was inert in her chair, occasionally dragging on the cigarette, occasionally pulling on the bottle. She seemed to have forgotten I was there. I had other questions, but I couldn't stand to ask them. I couldn't stand being there anymore. I turned and went to the door and stopped and looked back at her. She sat motionless, oblivious, her back to me, her face to the television.

I opened my mouth and couldn't think what to say and closed it, and went out into the putrid weed smell and walked back out Polton's Lane, trying not to breathe deeply.

23

FROM the Hyatt in Mission Bay, I called Mindy at the Zenith Meridien production office in Boston.

"The trail," I said, "leads to L.A., sweetheart."

"Are you doing Cary Grant?" she said.

"You got some smart mouth, sweetheart. No wonder you're not an executive."

"It's not a smart mouth that gets a girl ahead in this business, big guy."

"Cynicism will age you," I said.

"So will you. You want a hotel in L.A.?"

"Yes, please."

"Zenith always puts people up at the Westwood Marquis," Mindy said. "Okay with you?"

"I'll make do," I said.

"Okay. Corner Hilgard and LeConte, in Westwood Village."

"I'll find it," I said.

"Super sleuth," she said, and hung up.

I checked out of the Islandia and headed back up the freeway. Having a production coordinator wasn't bad. Maybe I should employ one. I needed a hotel reservation and airline bookings every two, three years. In between times she could balance my checkbook.

The drive from San Diego to L.A. is not much more interesting than the drive from L.A. to San Diego. While I drove, I thought about what I was doing. As usual I was blundering around and seeing what I could kick up. So far I'd kicked up a child and another significant other in Jill Joyce's life.

So what?

So I hadn't known that before.

So how's it help?

How the hell do I know?

The Westwood Marquis had flower gardens and two swimming pools and a muted lobby and served tea in the afternoon. All the rooms were suites. Zenith Meridien must be doing okay.

Everybody I saw in the lobby was slender and tended to Armani sport coats with the sleeves pushed up. I had on jeans and a sweatshirt with the sleeves cut off. My luggage was a gray gym bag with ADIDAS in large red letters along the side. I felt like a rhinoceros at a petting zoo.

I unpacked in my pale rose room and took a shower. Then I called an L.A. cop I knew named Samuelson and at 3:30 in the afternoon I was in my rental car heading downtown, on Wilshire.

The homicide bureau was located in the police building on Los Angeles Street. Samuelson's office looked like it had eight years ago when I was in there last. There was a desk, a file cabinet, an air conditioner under the window behind Samuelson's desk. The air conditioner was still noisy and there was still something wrong with the thermostat because it kept cycling on and shutting off as we talked. Samuelson appeared not to notice. He was a tall guy, nearly bald, with a droopy mustache and tinted aviator-style glasses. His corduroy jacket hung on a hook on a hat rack behind the door. Beyond the glass partition the homicide squad room spread out like squad rooms in every city. They all seemed to have been designed from the same blueprint.

"Probably a squad room on Jupiter," I said, "looks just like this."

Samuelson nodded. He had on a white shirt and a red and blue striped tie with the tie at half mast and the collar unbuttoned. He leaned back in his swivel chair and put his hands behind his head. He wore his gun high on his belt on the right side.

"Last time I saw you," Samuelson said, "you'd finished fucking up a case of ours."

"Always glad to help out," I said.

"So what do you need?" Samuelson said.

"I'd like to talk with a guy named Victor del Rio."

Samuelson showed no reaction.

"Yeah?" he said.

"He's not listed in the L.A. book," I said. "I was wondering if you had anything on him."

"Why do you want to talk with him?" Samuelson said.

"Would you buy, 'it's confidential'?"

"Would you buy, 'get lost'?"

"I'm backtracking on a murder in Boston; del Rio was once intimate with a figure in the case. He fathered her daughter."

"And the figure?" Samuelson was perfectly patient. He was used to asking. He learned everything he knew this way. One answer at a time, nothing volunteered. If he minded it didn't show.

"Jill Joyce," I said.

"TV star?"

"Un huh."

"You private guys get all the glamour work," Samuelson said. "She try to bang you yet?"

"Ah, you know Miss Joyce," I said.

Samuelson shrugged. "Victor del Rio runs the Hispanic rackets in L.A."

"That's heartwarming," I said. "A success story."

"Yeah, a big one," Samuelson said.

"So where do I find him?" I said.

"If you annoy del Rio you will be in bigger trouble than I can get you out of," Samuelson said.

"Why do you think I'll annoy him?" I said.

"Because you annoy me," Samuelson said. "And I'm a cupcake compared to del Rio. You got a gun?"

"Yes."

"You licensed in California?"

"No."

"Of course not," Samuelson said. "Del Rio's got a place in Bel Air."

"Not East L.A.?"

"Are you kidding," Samuelson said. "That's where he makes his money. It's not where he lives."

"You got an address?"

"Wait a minute," Samuelson said. He picked up the phone and spoke into it. Outside in the main squad room an L.A. cop with his handcuffs dangling from his shoulder holster was talking to an Hispanic kid wearing a bandanna wrapped around his head. The cop would lean forward every once in a while and tilt his head up to full face by chucking him firmly under the chin. The kid would hold the gaze for a moment and then his head would drop again.

Samuelson hung up and scribbled an address on a piece of paper. He handed me the paper.

"Off Stone Canyon Road, you know where that is?" he said.

"Yeah."

"Don't give del Rio a lot of lip," Samuelson said. "I'm overworked now."

I stood and tucked the address into my shirt pocket.

"Thanks," I said.

"I can't give you a lot of help with del Rio," Samuelson said. "He is very connected."

"Me too," I said. "Detective to the stars."

24

BEL Air had its own gate, opposite the point where Beverly Glen jogs on Sunset. There was a gatehouse and alert members of the Bel Air patrol in evidence. I went past the gate on Sunset and turned into Stone Canyon Road. There was no gate, no members of the private patrol. I was always puzzled why they bothered with the gatehouse. Stone Canyon Road wound through trees and crawling greenery all the way up to Mulholland Drive. I wasn't going that far. About a mile in I turned off the drive onto a side road and 100 yards farther I turned in between two beige brick pillars with huge wrought-iron lanterns on the top. I stopped. There was a big wrought-iron gate barring the way. Beyond the gate a black Mercedes sedan with tinted windows was parked. I let my car idle. On the other side of the gate the Mercedes idled. The temperature was ninety. Finally a guy got out of the passenger side of the Mercedes and walked slowly toward the gate. He wore a black silk suit of Italian cut and a white dress shirt buttoned to the neck, no tie. His straight black hair was slicked back in a ducktail, and his face had the strong-nosed look of an American Indian.

He stood on the inside of the gate and gestured at me. I nodded and got out of the car.

"Name's Spenser," I said. "I'm working on a case in Boston and I need to see Mr. del Rio."

"You got some kind of warrant, Buck?" His voice had a flat southwestern lilt to it. He spoke without moving his lips.

"Private cop," I said and handed him a business card through the gate. He didn't look at it. He simply shook his head at me.

"Vamoose," he said.

"Vamoose?"

"Un huh."

"Last time I heard someone say that was on Tom Mix and his Ralston Straight Shooters."

The Indian wasn't impressed. He gestured toward my car with his thumb, and turned and started away.

"Tell your boss it's about somebody named Zabriskie," I said.

The Indian stopped and turned around.

"Who the hell is Zabriskie," he said, "and why does Mr. del Rio care?"

"Ask him," I said. "He'll want to see me."

The Indian paused for a moment and pushed his lower lip out beyond his upper.

"Okay," he said, "but if you're horsing around with me I'm going to come out there and put your ass on the ground."

"You don't *sound* like a Ralston Straight Shooter," I said.

The Indian tapped on the window on the driver's

side. It rolled down silently. He spoke to the driver, and the driver handed him a phone. The Indian spoke on the phone again and waited, and spoke again. Then he listened. Then he handed the phone back inside the Mercedes and walked toward the gate. The gate swung open as he walked toward it.

"I'll ride up with you," he said.

"How nice," I said.

We got in my car and headed up the drive. The gate swung silently shut behind us. The roadway wound uphill through what looked like pasture land. Trees defined the borders of the property, but inside the borders was smooth lawn and green grass grew thickly under the steady sweep of a sprinkler system. To my left a young woman on a white horse came up over the crest of a low hill and reined in the horse and watched as the car went past. Then we came around another turn in the road and there was the house, a long, low structure with many wings that sprawled over the top of the next hill in a kind of undulating ramble. It was white stucco with the ends of the roof beams exposed.

"Park over there," the Indian said.

I put the rental car in a turnaround that was paved with crushed oyster shells and we got out and walked back toward the house. The Indian rang the doorbell.

We waited.

The front door was made to look as if it had been hammered together from old mesquite wood and had probably cost $5,000. The plantings along the foundation of the house were low and tasteful and tended to bright red flowers. I could smell the flowers, and the grass, and a hint of water flowing somewhere, and even fainter, a hint of the nearly sweet smell of horses. A Mexican guy opened the door. He was medium-sized and agile-looking with shoulder-length hair and a diamond stud in his ear. Behind him was another Mexican, bigger, bulkier, with a coat that fit too tight and a narrow tie that was knotted up tight to his thick neck.

Nobody said anything. The Indian turned and walked back toward my car. The graceful Mexican man nodded me into the house. Inside there was a large foyer with benches that looked like antique church pews on three walls. Three or four other Mexican men lounged on the benches. None of them looked like a poet. The slender Mexican made a gesture with his hands toward the wall, and I leaned against it while he patted me down. The bulky one stood and stared at me.

"Gun's under the left arm," I said.

Nobody said anything. The Mexican took my gun from my shoulder holster and handed it to the bulky guy. He stuck it in the side pocket of his plaid sport coat. The slender Mexican straightened and jerked his head for me to follow him. We went through an archway to the left and along a corridor that appeared to curve along the front of the house, like an enclosed veranda. We stopped at a door with a frosted glass window and the slender Mexican knocked and opened the door.

He nodded me through.

"Cat got your tongue?" I said.

He ignored me and came in behind me and closed the door. Through the frosted glass I could see the shadow of the bulky Mexican as he leaned against the wall outside.

Behind a bare wooden desk a man said, "What about Zabriskie?"

He looked like a stage Mexican. He had a thin droopy mustache and thick black hair that seemed uncombed and fell artfully over his forehead. He was wearing a Western-cut white shirt with billowy sleeves, and he was smoking a thin black cigar.

"You del Rio?" I said.

Behind the stage Mexican there was a low table, as plain as the desk. On it was a picture of an aristocratic-looking woman with black hair touched with gray, and beside it, a picture of a young woman, perhaps twenty, with olive skin and a strong resemblance to Jill Joyce. I was pretty sure I had a picture of her when she was younger, inside my coat pocket.

"I asked you a question, gringo."

"Ai chihuahua!" I said.

Del Rio smiled suddenly, his teeth very white under the silly mustache.

"Then Chollo here sings a couple of choruses of 'South of the Border,' " he said, "and we all have tortillas and drink some tequila. Si?"

"You got a guitar?" I said.

"The 'gringo' stuff impresses a lot of anglos," del Rio said. "Makes them think I'm very bad."

"Scared the hell out of me," I said.

"I can see that," del Rio said.

Chollo had gone to one side of the office and lounged in a green leather armchair, almost boneless in his relaxed slouch. His black eyes had no meaning in them.

"You see how we scared him, Chollo?" del Rio said.

"I could improve on it, Vic, if you want." It was the first time he'd spoken. Neither he nor del Rio had even a hint of an accent.

"You sure you guys are Mexican?" I said.

"Straight from Montezuma," del Rio said. "Me and Chollo both. Pure blood line. What's this about Zabriskie?"

I took the picture out of my inside pocket and put it in front of del Rio. He looked at it without touching it. I picked it up again and put it back in my pocket.

"So?" del Rio said.

"Your daughter," I said.

Del Rio didn't speak.

"I got it from her grandmother."

Del Rio waited.

"Anything you don't want him to know?" I said.

"Chollo knows what I know," del Rio said. "Chollo's family."

"How nice for Chollo," I said. "I know who your daughter's mother is."

"Yes?"

"Jill Joyce," I said, "America's cutie."

"She tell you that?" del Rio said.

"No," I said. "She hasn't told me anything, and half of that is lies."

Del Rio nodded.

"That would be Jill," he said. "What do you want?"

"Information," I said. "It's like huevos rancheros to a detective."

"Si," del Rio said.

"Were you and Jill married?" I said.

Del Rio leaned back a little in his chair with his hands resting quietly on the bare desk top in front of him. His nails were manicured. I waited.

"Your name is Spenser," he said.

I nodded.

"Okay, Spenser. You think you're a tough guy. I can tell. I see a lot of people who think they are a tough guy. You probably are a tough guy. You got the build for it. But if I just nod at Chollo you are a dead guy. You understand? Just nod, and . . ." He made an out sign, jerking his left thumb toward his shoulder.

"Yikes," I said.

"So you know," del Rio said, "you're on real shaky ground here."

"It goes no further than me," I said.

"Maybe it doesn't go that far," del Rio said. "Why are you nosing around in my life in the first place?"

"I'm working on a murder in Boston," I said. "And I'm working on protecting Jill Joyce. The two things seem to be connected and your name popped up."

"Long way from Boston," del Rio said.

"Not my fault. Somebody has been threatening Jill Joyce. Someone killed her stunt double. Jill won't tell me anything about herself, so I started looking and I found her mother and then I found you."

Del Rio looked at me again in silence.

"Okay, Spenser. I met Jill Joyce when she was Jillian Zabriskie and she was trying to be an actress, and I was starting to build my career. We were together awhile. She got pregnant. I had a wife. She didn't want the kid, but she figured it would give her a hold on me. Even then I had a little clout. So she had it and left it with her mother. I got her some parts. She slept with some producers. I supported the kid."

"You still got the same wife?"

"Yes. Couple years after Amanda was born, Jill's mother started disappearing into the sauce. She was never much, but . . ." He shrugged. The shrug was eloquent. It was the first genuine Latin gesture I'd seen. "So my wife and I adopted her."

"Your wife know about you and Jill?"

"No."

"She know you're the kid's father?"

"No. She thinks we adopted her from an orphanage. We don't have any other children."

"How old is Amanda now?"

"Twenty."

"What happens if your wife finds out?"

"Whoever told her dies."

"What happens to her?"

Again the eloquent shrug. "My wife is Catholic," del Rio said. "She is a lady. She would feel humiliated and betrayed. I won't let that happen."

"Amanda know?"

"No."

We all were silent then, while we thought about these things.

"And Jill knows better than to talk about this," I said.

"Jill don't want to talk about it. Jill don't want anyone to know she got a spic baby."

"But if someone was looking into things you might want to squelch that," I said.

"I wanted to, I would," del Rio said.

"What if you sent some soldier out there to clip her and he got the wrong one," I said.

"Get you killed," del Rio said, "thinking things like that."

I nodded. "Something will, sooner or later," I said.

"Most people prefer later," del Rio said.

We all thought a little more.

"I don't like you for it," I said. "It's too stupid. Killing Jill or somebody else like that stirs up more trouble than it squashes. You'd know that."

"Haven't killed you yet," del Rio said.

"Same reason," I said. "You don't know who knows I'm here."

"You gotta understand something, Spenser." He

always pronounced my name as if it were in quotes. "I'm a bad guy. Maybe the baddest in southern California. But bad guys maybe have good sides too."

"Hitler loved dogs," I said. "I hear he was sentimental."

"I love my wife. I love my daughter. I'm going to protect them—their privacy, their dignity, all of it. And if that means killing some people, I'm bad enough for that. And if it means not killing people I ought to kill, I'm all right there too."

"Okay," I said. "I buy it. What you told me is between us."

"If it isn't, you're dead."

"It is, but not because you might kill me," I said, ". . . if you can."

Del Rio frowned at me for a moment, then his face cleared.

"No," he said. "It's probably not."

"What can you tell me about Jill?" I said.

Del Rio gestured toward the other green leather chair, the only other piece of furniture in the office.

"I'll tell you what I know," he said.

25

CHOLLO was still draped in the chair like a dead snake. The shadow of the bulky Mexican was still motionless outside the door. I was in the other chair, sitting in it backwards with my forearms folded over the back. It had grown dark outside the office and del Rio hadn't turned on a light, so we all sat in the aftermath of sunset as del Rio talked.

"She was already starting to get a little attention," del Rio said. "She had that face, and the body . . . eighteen years old, maybe. The face says *I'm an angel,* and the body says, *The hell I am.* We were at a fund raiser for barrio kids." Del Rio paused to laugh softly. "Nobody there ever been to the barrio, except me. I was the most important barrio graduate they could find . . . and I was a crook." He laughed again. "It was a fashion show, and the models were supposed to be well-known actresses and TV people, but mostly they were kids like Jill. She tagged on to me. She didn't have much class, she didn't know how to act, but she had a quality." He shrugged. "I'm very loyal to my wife. I love her. I admire her. She's not part of my business, she's got nothing to do with that world. She lives in another one. I live there sometimes too. But in the business world I snack now and then . . . still do. It's got nothing to do with her. Nothing to do with her world. You understand?"

I shrugged.

"Don't matter if you understand or not," he said. "Jill was just another snack. Except for that quality."

He paused again and thought about the quality. I waited.

"We were together maybe a year. Always careful, never embarrass my wife, but when she had the kid she started to turn the screw a little."

Again he paused and thought about things. Again I waited.

"I'm not a good man to pressure; but this came close to the other world, if you follow me, and there was the kid. Whatever else she was, Jill was my kid's mother. I couldn't just have her clipped. So I supported the kid, and I went to see her when I could. It didn't take long to see where it was headed. You've seen Jill's old lady."

I nodded.

"I got lawyers, I talked with my wife. I said there was a girl, daughter of one of my people. I said her father died, her mother didn't want her. I said I wanted to adopt her. My wife is very proud. It was always a loss to her that she couldn't have kids . . ." He spread his hands.

I nodded.

"We raised her careful. She went to school with the nuns. Goes to school now in Geneva. She plays the piano, speaks French perfect. Maybe you saw her when you came up the drive. Riding a white horse. Can ride like a jockey."

I nodded.

"I bought her that white horse for her sixteenth birthday. From school she writes it letters. Her mother reads them to the horse."

Del Rio looked at me hard for a moment. I made no comment.

"She's home for Christmas," he said.

I nodded. To my left Chollo got up and squatted before the fireplace on the left wall. He fiddled with it for a moment while del Rio and I watched. Then a gas flame appeared. Chollo put a couple of dry, barkless logs on top of the grate and stood and went back to his chair. The blue gas flame began to move among the logs, turning orange where it hit them and caught.

"So I told Jill," del Rio said, "I take care of the kid. The kid is mine. She is no longer yours. She belongs to me and to my wife. My wife is her mother now. I said if she ever caused me trouble, if she ever hurt my daughter or my wife, if she ever spoke of this . . ."

Del Rio held his right hand out, with the first two fingers apart like the blades of a scissors, and closed them. Nobody said anything. The flame had caught the bone-dry wood and made bright heatless orange movements in the Mexican tile fireplace. A California fire. All light, no heat.

"Jill never really had any luck," del Rio said. He was sitting back in his chair now, his hands locked behind his head, staring into the fire. "Sounds funny to say about her. She's a big star, big TV star. But she's never really caught a break . . . except me."

Del Rio paused again. I could hear him breathing softly through his nose.

"I got her started. She came from nowhere. Mother's a drunk. Old man left when she was a kid. Had a baby, had to give it up. She never knew what she was, then she got to be a star and everybody started treating her like she was a princess, you know . . . the fucking emperor's daughter . . . so she thought she was."

"She knows she isn't," I said.

Del Rio shifted his eyes to me thoughtfully.

"Maybe," he said. "Maybe she does."

"Makes it worse," I said.

Del Rio nodded slowly with the right side of his face lit by the fire and the left side in darkness.

"Si," he said.

26

JILL'S agent worked for an agency that occupied the top half of a new skyscraper in Century City where, if you looked out the windows, you could see Twentieth Century Fox. While I sat in the waiting room two would-be starlets with flat blue eyes and a lot of blond hair chanted at the switchboard.

"Robert Brown Agency, good morning."

Each of them said it maybe a hundred times while I waited. Each time they said it exactly as they had said it previously. Then they would listen and touch a button and the call would be processed. There was a mindless fascination to it, like watching water boil. The waiting room was done in beige marble and pale green carpeting. On the wall above the blond bentwood chair I sat in was a picture of the founder of the agency. Robert Brown had a wide face and red cheeks, and the smile of a child molester. Under the portrait was a brass plaque bearing his name and the single word INTEGRITY.

On some of the other chairs sat people trying to look in control while they waited hopefully. There was a guy in a silk tweed jacket and starched jeans carrying a manila envelope that reeked of manuscript. He had no socks on, and his ankles were tan above the low cut of his woven leather loafers. Under the silk tweed he wore a tuxedo shirt, open at the throat. Agents, mostly men, mostly young, strolled through the waiting room to and from the inner spaces, carrying themselves as insiders always did in the presence of outsiders.

A good-looking young woman with more hair than the switchboard ladies came out from one of the doors behind the switchboard. She wore a cobalt silk dress spattered with red flowers. Her hips rolled as she walked.

"Mr. Spenser?" she said. Her eyes sparkled, her smile gleamed.

I nodded.

"Hi, I'm Jasmine, Ken's assistant. Ken's on the phone long distance to London and he asked me to see if you wanted coffee or anything."

"Hot diggity," I said.

Jasmine's smile gleamed even more brightly.

"Excuse me?" she said.

"London is exciting," I said. "I mean, how would I feel if you came out and said I'd have to wait because Ken was on the phone to Culver City?"

Jasmine seemed a bit confused, but it in no way interfered with the luminosity of her smile.

"Exactly," she said. "Did you say you wanted coffee?"

"No, thank you, Jasmine."

"Tea, juice, Perrier?"

"No, thank you, Jasmine."

"Well, you be comfortable, and Ken will be with you as soon as he can get off the phone."

"Sure," I said.

Jasmine rolled her hips away from me, walking with a long stride on high heels which emphasized her natural wiggle. I waited. Behind the switchboard operators was a floor-to-ceiling picture window for looking at Twentieth Century. On either side were doors that opened into the working spaces of the Robert Brown Agency, where clients and agents conspired on who knows what unspeakable project. A fat woman with extensive make-up came in carrying an animal that looked like a fluffy rat. She was wearing a fur coat, though when I'd come in a half hour ago the temperature at Century City had been eighty-seven. Her hair in its natural state was probably brown turning gray. In its present state, however, it was the color of a lemon, and stiff with hair spray so thick that you could cut yourself on her curls. She spoke inaudibly to one of the switchboard operators, then took up a seat with the fluffy rat on her lap, and gazed at the room before her the way Marie Antoinette must have gazed at the crowds in Paris. The small white animal wiggled out of her lap and waded through the pale green carpet and stood in front of me and began to yap. It was a persistent high yap that had the same metronomic quality that the ladies of the switchboard displayed.

"Oh, Beenie," the fat blonde said, "stop that noise right now."

Beenie paid her no heed at all.

"He won't hurt you," the blonde said.

"That's for sure," I said.

The blonde looked startled. "Well, he won't. He's usually very good with strangers."

The yaps continued. It was a piercing sound. Even the two switchboard receptionists turned glazed eyes toward the sound.

"What kind of rat is this?" I said politely.

"Rat?" The blonde's voice went up an octave in the middle. Not easy to do in a one-syllable word.

"Oh, I'm sorry," I said. "Of course he's not a rat. Guinea pig maybe?"

"You fucking creep," the blonde said.

Jasmine appeared radiantly at the door. She frowned a little, but only for a moment, at the yapping and the "fucking creep" and then smiled even more brilliantly than before and said, "Ken can see you now, Mr. Spenser."

I scooped up the yapping animal and dropped it into the blonde's lap as I headed for the office door.

"Spenser," she said. "I'll remember that name."

I smiled my killer smile at her. She remained calm. I followed Jasmine through the door. I went down the long corridor lined with glass-partitioned cubicles. At the end was a bigger office, with real walls as befits a senior agent representing the highest TVQ in the industry. He stood and walked around his desk, a tall elegant man in a double-breasted blazer and a soft white shirt. He had the kind of tan that would soon lead to basal cell carcinoma, and his dark hair, touched with gray at the temples, was combed back in easy waves, longish in the back. His grip was firm as we shook hands.

"Ken Craig," he said. "Really glad to meet you."

There was a faintly British sound to his speech, either long forgotten or recently cultivated, I couldn't tell which. His office was done in the same beige and green tones and the walls were covered with abstract art which lent color, but no meaning, to his surroundings. It was a corner office and you could look at the Twentieth Century lot from two different angles.

"Please," Craig said, and gestured toward an armchair done in pale peach. I sat. "I know you're helping Jill out with that trouble in Boston," he said. "How can I help?"

"Tell me a little about her, Mr. Craig."

"About Jill? Well . . . brilliant talent, truly. And a real pro. A pleasure to work with. I consider Jilly not only a client but a friend."

"No," I said, "I'm talking about Jill Joyce, the former Jillian Zabriskie."

"I beg your pardon?"

I put my left ankle over my right knee and laced my fingers behind my head. My New Balance running shoes were getting a little ratty. If I was going to be in show business I might have to spring for some new ones.

"I've worked with her too, Mr. Craig."

"Ken."

"And I know what you must know . . . that she's an imperial pain in the ass."

Craig stared at me politely for a moment and then his face slowly creased into a smile.

"Of course she is," he said. "But she is also the number one television star in these United States."

"Which means she's a valuable commodity."

"Exactly," Craig said.

"So tell me about her as, what we investigators like to call, a person."

Craig frowned.

"You know, what's she like? What causes her pain? What gives her happiness?" I said. "Talk about her not as a client but as a friend."

Craig continued to frown. "I don't . . ." he said and paused and seemed to be trying to regroup. "I don't really think . . . ah . . ."

"These questions too hard for you, Ken?"

"Well, perhaps I shouldn't, you know. Perhaps I'm not at liberty . . ."

"Perhaps you don't know," I said. I could feel the telltale stirring in the trapezius muscles. I was tiring of the television business. "Perhaps that stuff about her being client and friend was bullshit, and you don't know how to say anything that isn't bullshit."

"Wait just a minute," Ken said. "I'm responsible for Jill's professional life. Her personal life is hers."

"You ever meet her family?"

Craig looked surprised. "No," he said. "I didn't know she had any."

"Un huh."

"Well, that's not quite true. She has a father. I met him once."

"Run into him at Spago?" I said.

Craig snorted. "Hardly," he said. "He came here once. Looking for money, as I recall. Said he couldn't get a response from Jill. We ushered him out, politely."

"What did he want the money for?" I said.

"Down and out, I assume. He didn't look very successful."

"What was his name?" I said.

"Zabriskie, ah, Bill, Bill Zabriskie."

"He live around here?"

"I don't know," Craig said. "I assume he lives somewhere in Los Angeles."

"You have any thoughts on why someone would threaten Jill, or harass her, or attempt to kill her?"

"Certainly no one in the industry," Craig said. "She's a television money machine."

"The industry," I said.

"Yeah, you know, the business."

"Of course," I said. "How about motives other than money?"

"Such as?" Craig said.

"I know this is hard," I said, "but maybe passion, jealousy, rage, unrequited love, unrequited lust, revenge, stuff like that."

"Well," Craig was thinking carefully, "Jill, as you pointed out, can be difficult."

"Like life itself," I said. "What do you think? Any

disgruntled lovers, angry suitors, any history of wacko fans? Anything that might help?"

"I'm sorry, Mr. Spenser, I really can't be much help. Jill's a wonderful girl and I love her madly, but . . ." He shrugged. "I try to keep my clients' private affairs separate from our professional relationship."

"But you know her TVQ," I said.

"I resent that," Craig said.

"I don't care."

"What makes you think you're some kind of East Coast tough guy can walk in here and insult me?"

"I *am* some kind of East Coast tough guy," I said. "And a man would have to have a heart of stone not to insult you."

"You better just watch your step, pal," Craig said. He stood up as he said it and looked as menacing as the angora rat that had yapped at me in his waiting room.

"That's the problem with you television guys," I said. "You have no sense of reality. Look at me. Look at you. Consider the plausibility of standing up and telling me to watch my step."

Craig stared at me for a moment, then he pressed the button on his intercom and said, "Jasmine. Would you come in here and show Mr. Spenser out, please."

"Ah," I said, "at last a worthy adversary."

Jasmine came in, smiled at me like a klieg light and held the door open. I started out.

"When we go through the waiting room, Jasmine, try to stay between me and that savage guinea pig."

"I'll be with you," Jasmine said, "every step of the way."

27

THERE were seven Zabriskies in the L.A. books, but only one William. I tried him first and he was the one. He lived in an apartment building in Hollywood, on Vermont Avenue, south of Franklin. It was built during what L.A. thinks are the old days, around 1932, under the impression that it was going to be a Moorish palace. It was named The Balmoral and it was built in a squat U shape around an open courtyard with a fountain in the middle that didn't work. There were architectural curlicues along the entire top of the building and each window had a white marble lintel set into the brown stucco. Most of the windows were open in the heat and here and there a dirty curtain fluttered wanly in the languid air. Occasionally there was a fan, and an air conditioner protruded from one window. A sidewalk of concrete stairs led through the center of the courtyard, Y'd around the dry fountain and led to the glass front door, which had chipped gilt letters that said THE BALMORAL. Some newspapers, still rolled, were yellowing inside the doorway. There were a few tired-looking yucca trees declining on either side, and the vestiges of untended plantings scrabbled for life on the hard-baked soil of the courtyard. It smelled hot, and it sounded hot with the slow drone of insects amplified by the three enclosing walls. Through the open windows I could hear a television playing. The door was supposed to lock automatically, but the frame was warped and the door didn't close tight. I pushed it open and went in. I was wearing a light sport coat to hide my gun. It felt like a mackinaw in the glassed-in entry. I could feel the sweat begin to form along my backbone and trickle down. William Zabriskie was listed on the first floor, number 103. I went into the lobby; it was littered with discarded junk mail and reeked with heat. Once it had been ornate, with carved wood paneling and marble floors. The paneling was warped now, with its oak veneer peeling off. The marble floors were deeply stained and there were dried yucca leaves in the corners. I stood for a moment in the silent stifling lobby. It was old. The building was old. The yucca leaves in the corner were old. The two-color flyers for supermarket sales seemed as if they were probably there when the building was built. The windows across from the door were shut and looked as if they wouldn't open. No air stirred. The light filtering through the windows was grayed by its passage through the dirt on the windows. What light got through highlighted the dust motes that moped in the still air.

"Old," I said. My voice was harsh in the heavy stillness.

I went down the acrid, dingy corridor and knocked on number 103. When the door opened I felt the faint stir of air from an open window inside. Zabriskie was a tall old man with no shirt. He wasn't fat, but age had made his muscles sag and the skin hung loose and dry as parchment beneath the thin scatter of gray hair on his chest. His hair was gray too, longish and combed straight back all around. He was still handsome, though the line along his jaw had blurred, and there was too much skin around his eyes so that he seemed heavy-lidded. He seemed familiar until I realized that Jill took after him. He was wearing white polyester pants—the kind that don't take a belt and close by a buttoned tab over the middle. On his feet he had woven sandals. He looked at me without comment, his eyebrows raised a little in inquiry. I gave him my card.

"I'm working on a case involving Jill Joyce," I said. "I understand you're her father."

"From whom?" he said. *Whom.*

"Several sources," I said. "May I come in?"

Zabriskie hesitated a moment, then backed away from the door and nodded for me to enter.

The apartment was neat. The lace curtains stirring listlessly in the faint-hearted air from the open window were white. There was a living room, a kitchenette, and a bedroom. Through a door that was partially ajar, I could see the hospital corner of a neatly made bed. In the living room was a couch with plaid upholstery and wooden arms. A chair matched it. There was a foot locker in front of the couch with some magazines in a neat pile, and a small lace doily. Clean dishes rested in the drainer on the counter next to the kitchen sink.

I sat in the plaid chair. My shirt was soaked through and my jacket was nearly so. If I didn't find air conditioning soon my gun would rust.

"So why have you come to see me," Zabriskie said carefully.

"I'd like to talk with you about your daughter."

"No," he said. "Don't speak of her that way. Call her Jill Joyce."

"Why?" I said.

"Because I wish it so," he said.

"Besides that," I said.

"She never speaks of me as her father," he said.

"You left when she was pretty young," I said.

"I left her mother," Zabriskie said. "Any man would have."

"You stay in touch with Jill?"

"I tried. Her mother interfered. After a time I stopped trying. But I was always there for her."

"Did she know that?"

He shrugged. Hot as it was there was no sweat on him.

"A father is available to his child," he said.

"Though the child may not necessarily know that," I said.

"I am here for her now," he said.

"You ever see her?" I said.

"I see her often," Zabriskie said. "On the television."

"Does she ever see you?" I said.

"No."

Zabriskie sat perfectly still.

"When's the last time she saw you?" I said.

"Nineteen fifty-five," he said.

"She would have been how old?"

"She was four. It was her fourth birthday. I gave her a present—a stuffed cat—and I kissed her on the forehead and said good-bye and left."

"And you haven't, ah, she hasn't seen you since."

"No," Zabriskie said.

"But you've been there for her if she needed you, all this time?"

"Yes," Zabriskie said.

I wiped my forehead with the back of my hand. It didn't clear the sweat but it smeared it around for a moment.

"Did you remarry?" I said.

"Yes," Zabriskie said. He smiled. "Three more wives," he said.

"You don't have any idea why someone would wish to hurt her?"

"Jill?"

"Yes."

"No. Jill is a lovely girl, and very successful."

I nodded. I rolled my lower lip over my upper one. It wasn't much but it was all I could think of to do.

"Still married?" I said.

"Not at the moment," Zabriskie said.

I did my trick with the lower lip again. Spenser, master interrogator, never at a loss.

"Okay," I said. "Well, thanks a lot, Mr. Zabriskie."

I stood up.

"You're welcome," Zabriskie said. He stood up.

I walked to the door and opened it. I smiled at him. He smiled at me. Serenely. I went out. He closed the door.

28

I STOOD in Forest Lawn Cemetery and looked down at the marker. Candace Sloan, it said. B. 1950 D. 1981. The headstones stretched out around me in all directions, measuring the green sweep of the hillside. Behind me the rental car was parked on the drive. My suitcase was in it with the big red letters spelling ADIDAS on the side. In an hour and a half I'd be flying to Boston. In six or seven hours I'd be with Susan.

There were flowers at many of the grave sites. And there were a few other people looking at gravestones the way I was. The only sound was the swish of the water sprinklers as they arched repetitiously over the green grass; and, more distantly, the sound of traffic on the Ventura Freeway; and, over all, the hard silence—made more resounding by the hints of punctuation.

I could feel the high hot California sun on the back of my neck as I stood with my hands in my hip pockets staring down at Candy's grave. I hadn't been there for the funeral. The last time I'd seen her was in a degenerating oil field, faceup in a hard rain with the blood washing pinkish off her face.

I pursed my lips a little.

Above us the sky was bright blue. There were a few white clouds and they were moving very lazily west toward the Pacific. Some sort of bird chittered somewhere. On the freeway a truck shifted gears on a grade. Still I stared down at the grass in front of the headstone. She wasn't there. Whatever there was of her there didn't matter. She probably wasn't anywhere. I looked up and back, toward the Valley and beyond the Valley, toward the mountains. There wasn't any smog today, and the snowcaps on some of the highest peaks were clear to see, white above the clay color of the mountains.

None of the stuff that anyone had ever written seemed useful. I had nothing much to offer either. The bird chittered again. Above me the clouds drifted west, and the sun imperceptibly followed. The sky stayed blue, the earth below stayed green. I looked again briefly at the gravestone and blew out my breath once, and turned and walked back toward my rental car.

"Some bodyguard," I said, and even though I spoke softly, my voice sounded very loud in the still burial ground and the words seemed to hang there as I drove away.

29

REALITY again. Outside Quirk's office, looking down into an alley off Stanhope Street, the temperature was maybe fifteen. The grime-streaked snow was packed like concrete in the rutted areas where the plows couldn't get because there were always cars. Inside Quirk's office was Marty Riggs, the big executive from Zenith Meridien. He had hung up his long scarf. He was holding forth intensely to an audience composed of Quirk; me; Sandy Salzman; Milo Nogarian, the executive producer; Herb Brodkey, a lawyer for Zenith; and Morris Callahan, a lawyer for the network.

"Who the hell was guarding her?" Riggs said. He was every inch the captain of a damaged ship, angry and indomitable in the face of near disaster.

"Spenser assured us the guy was very good," Salzman said.

I looked at Quirk. His face was expressionless. He was carefully looking at a paper clip, manipulating it in his fingers, apparently trying to straighten it out with only one hand.

"Well, where is he? He's so good, why isn't he here?"

Quirk glanced at me and smiled faintly. Riggs saw him.

"Something amusing you, Lieutenant?"

"Whether Hawk's good enough hasn't got anything to do with whether Hawk's here, if you see what I mean. It's, you might say, ah . . ." He revolved his hand at me to fill in.

"Non sequitur," I said.

"Don't get cute with me, Lieutenant. This is your case and so far you haven't shown me anything."

"Actually, Mr. Riggs, it's not my case. You asked for this meeting, and being a courteous person and a dedicated public servant, I agreed. But my case is who killed your stunt woman. What happened to your star is missing persons—unless she turns up dead."

"Bureaucracy," Riggs said. "Herb, I told you we should have arranged a meeting with the commissioner."

Brodkey looked like Fernando Lamas. He had a rich tan and his nails gleamed. He had probably last been in criminal court when they indicted Fatty Arbuckle. He made a placating gesture at Riggs.

"I understand you've interviewed the bodyguard," Brodkey said.

"Sergeant Belson did," Quirk said. "He knows Hawk. It's easier that way."

"Is this man getting special treatment?" Riggs snapped.

"Not like you are," Quirk said softly.

"This is a difficult case, Lieutenant. Just tell us

what you know." It was Callahan, the network lawyer. He had white hair and a big nose and the look of a man eager to get the 7:30 shuttle back to New York. Even if it was on time there was still the ride to Greenwich.

"Hawk took Miss Joyce back to the hotel as usual," Quirk said. "It was about six-fifteen. He sat with her while she had a couple of drinks in the bar, and then he started to turn her over to hotel security. But she insisted that he take her up to her room himself. When he did she went in and left the door ajar. He started to close it when she screamed. Hawk went into the room, and when he did she closed the door and stood in front of it and laughed and said she wanted to see what he'd do if she screamed."

Quirk looked at me. "It is, I understand, a ploy she's used in the past."

No one said anything.

"Miss Joyce then insisted that Hawk make love to her. He declined, courteously he says." Again Quirk looked at me. I didn't say anything. "She was starting to disrobe," Quirk said.

"In front of the goddamned buck nigger?" Riggs said.

"His name's Hawk," I said.

"Well, what are we, touchy?"

"Call him Hawk," I said.

"I'll call him what I goddamned please," Riggs said. "I've got more to take up with you later."

"Call him Hawk," I said, "or I will bounce your

ass down two flights of stairs and out onto Berkeley Street."

"You heard that, Lieutenant? You heard him threaten me."

"Call him Hawk," Quirk said. He kept his gaze on Riggs for a moment and no one spoke. Then Quirk continued. "Hawk was apparently sincere in his disinterest. While she was disrobing he moved her forcibly but, ah, graciously, as I understand it, from the door and left. He told hotel security on his way out that they had her for the night, and he went home."

Quirk looked around the room. Riggs was still angry and struggling to find circumstances in which he could be commanding. The lawyers sat like lawyers, being careful. Salzman was leaning back in his chair, his legs out before him, his arms folded across his chest.

"Sometime that night, she left the hotel. Probably went out the back door, down the steps to University Road, to dodge the Cambridge prowl car out front, cut through JFK Park, walked up to Harvard Square. She got a cab near the Harvard Coop. He took her to Boston, to the Four Seasons Hotel. Said he dropped her off there about 10:00 P.M. She registered, under her own name, gave them an American Express card and went upstairs. She had no luggage. In the morning she had breakfast sent up about quarter to seven, and that's the last anyone has seen of her."

"And you have failed totally to find a single clue as to where she might be," Riggs said.

"Completely," Quirk said without expression.

"Do you have any idea who Jill Joyce is, Lieutenant? What she means to the American public? The amount of money her absence costs?"

"Save it for missing persons, Mr. Riggs," Quirk said. "I do murders."

"Goddamned bureaucrat," Riggs said only half aloud.

Quirk had been tipped back in his chair. He let it tip slowly forward and put his hands very lightly on the top of his desk.

"You are a very big deal in the TV business," Quirk said, "and the governor thinks you're the cat's ass, and I've been trying to help out because there's been a lot of heavy hitters juicing your case. But you are not a big deal in the Boston Police Department. I am. And I don't think you're the cat's ass. So you either shut your trap or I'll make you go sit in the corridor until the grown-ups are through."

Riggs' mouth opened like a carp. He seemed like he was having trouble getting his breath. He looked at the lawyers. Neither looked at him.

"I'll speak to your superiors," Riggs mumbled. But there was no heart in it.

"Good," Quirk said. "They like that. Gives them something to do." He looked at me. "You talk with Hawk?"

"No. I just came in from the, ah, coast last night."

"How nice for us," Quirk said. "You have anything to offer on this thing?"

"She wouldn't go alone," I said.

"No?"

"No. She needed somebody to take care of her, and it needed to be male. She might have scooted out alone, but she'd have had to know that a man was going to be around somewhere."

"What do you think?" Quirk said to Salzman.

Salzman shrugged. "I make film," he said. "I'm in so far over my head with the rest of this stuff that I don't know which way is up."

"Who's got this in missing persons?" I said.

"Lipsky," Quirk said. "I'm hanging around because it might be connected to the murder investigation."

I nodded.

"You talked about Jill Joyce with Susan?" Quirk said.

"Sure," I said.

"This theory about a man, Susan buy that?"

"Haven't asked her," I said. "Last night when I came home we barely spoke of Jill Joyce."

"Hard to imagine," Quirk said.

"Didn't even know she was gone," I said.

"We called L.A., yesterday morning," Salzman said. "Hotel said you'd checked out."

"I suppose you'll be looking for her too," Quirk said.

I nodded.

"Lipsky will be pleased to know he's not alone on this," Quirk said.

"Like you," I said.

"Just like me," Quirk said.

30

HAWK and I were in the boxing room at the Harbor Health Club. We were pretty much the only ones that ever went in there. There were people waiting to get on the stair climbers and bicycles and treadmills. There were platoons of young women with body stockings and water bottles in constant rotation on the chrome weight machines. But in the boxing room there was only Hawk and me and now and then Henry Cimoli, when he wasn't conferring with some stockbroker on the best way to sculpt the gluteus maximi. On the wall was a picture of Henry in his boxing shorts, taken the year after he'd fought Willie Pep. It was Henry's connection to his roots, that the boxing room still existed at the club. When Hawk and I started, it had been a gym, and as times changed and Henry changed with them it had turned into a health club and spa. Hawk and I still went there because of Henry, and Henry didn't charge us. But all of us remembered the times when you couldn't get an herbal wrap where you worked out.

I was hitting combination cycles on the heavy bag, and Hawk was playing the speed bag, whistling soundlessly the way he did. I don't think he needed to work on hand speed. I think he just liked the sound.

"We wouldn't be in this mess," I said, "if you'd just come across for her."

"Man's got standards," Hawk said. The speed bag rattled musically against the backboard.

"I didn't know you had standards," I said. I did two left jabs and an overhand right on the body bag. "I knew you insisted they be alive . . ."

"So how come you didn't give her a jab?" Hawk said. He was wearing a pair of violet silk sweat pants and white Avia basketball shoes. He had no shirt on and the muscles in his upper body coiled and uncoiled under his sweat-shiny black skin like liquid. The speed gloves he wore were red and when he hit the speed bag his hands were a red blur.

"I am," I said, "part of a fulfilling monogamous relationship."

"Holy shit," Hawk said.

"I knew you'd just forgotten that for a moment," I said. "What's your excuse?"

Hawk paused for a moment and picked up a towel and wiped off his face and head. I stopped too and got a drink from the cooler of spring water. Everyone in all health clubs had simultaneously decided that municipal water was undrinkable.

"Strange babe," Hawk said.

"Yeah."

"Most broads want to fuck me for the usual reasons," Hawk said. " 'Cause I'm handsome, manly, and slicker than goose shit."

"Or because they want to get even with their husbands, or they were just separated and want to prove they're still attractive," I said.

"Or because they heard about how once you go black you never go back," Hawk said.

"I never believed that one," I said.

"But Jill." Hawk shook his head. "Jill wants to fuck me for reasons got nothing to do with me, got nothing to do with pleasure. Jill wants to fuck me 'cause I'm black and it be a bad thing to do, you follow?"

"Sure," I said. "Help her feel bad about herself."

"Un huh," Hawk said.

"But it'd help her feel comfortable with you," I said. "If you'd tag somebody as bad as she is, you're not such a big deal either, and if she can get you to do it, then she's still got the power, the only one she can count on."

"Sigmund Spenser," Hawk said.

"You think I'm wrong?"

Hawk grinned and did a paradiddle on the speed bag.

"Think you right on target," he said. "You got no natural moves like me, but you learn pretty good."

"So where'd she go?" I said.

"Meet some man," Hawk said.

"That's the easy part," I said. Hawk began again on the speed bag. "Which man? Where?"

"You know some of the men in her life," Hawk said.

"That's about all there were," I said.

"Check them out."

I was hooking the heavy bag, three left hooks, one right. The bag bounced and swayed on the heavy chain. The shock of the punches went up my forearms. It had been one of my first surprises when I began to box, all that long time ago, punches hurt the wrists and forearms, you have to build up both to hit hard. Until you build them up you get not only arm weary, but arm sore.

"Cops are doing that," I said. "They got more manpower and clout than I have. They can do it quicker."

"They know all the names?" Hawk said.

"Sure," I said. "Almost."

"Figured you'd get sentimental 'bout one or two people."

"Guy out in the Berkshires, be too tough on him," I said. "Besides, she wouldn't go with him."

"Un huh."

"Guy in L.A., married, he wouldn't have her."

"Un huh." Hawk moved around the speed bag, hitting it in changing combinations like a man playing an instrument. "Maybe she threaten to tell the wife," he said.

"She's not that crazy," I said.

"Bad man?"

"He'd take Joe Broz with a Q-tip."

"Hell," Hawk said, "we can do that."

I hit the bag.

"I don't think she's that crazy," I said.

"She pretty crazy," Hawk said.

We both worked on our punches for a bit. The room was hot, there was light coming in through an ocean-facing window, and dust motes danced in its bright stream. Outside there were people tightening the upper abs, expanding the cardiovascular piping, firming up the pecs. In here there were only two guys beating hell out of simulated opponents. It seemed sort of silly, in that perspective. But it felt good.

"I was wondering," I said, when we were finished and the hot water was sluicing over us in the shower room, "how come you're so sure she went amok when you turned her down."

Hawk raised his head and stared at me.

"You can't be serious," he said.

31

I HAD my feet up on the window sill in my office. Across the way they had torn down the building where Linda Thomas had once worked. I used to watch her through the window, bent over her art board, then she'd been in my life, then she'd been gone. She was still gone, and now the building was gone. Sic transit the whole caboodle.

The phone rang behind me on the desk. I swiveled and answered. It was Quirk.

"Got a possible suicide you might be interested in," he said. "I'll pick you up outside your office in about two minutes."

"Okay," I said and hung up.

I had on my down-lined leather jacket and my Chicago Cubs baseball hat and was on the corner of Berkeley and Boylston with more than a minute to spare when Frank Belson wheeled the gray Chevy in toward me and backed up traffic on the green light while I climbed in the back. Belson hit the siren through the intersection and left it on.

"Cuts right through the holiday traffic," Belson said.

"Can't you get one that plays 'Silent Night'?" I said. "Whoop whoop just isn't jolly-sounding."

"Security guard saw a car go into the water off the pier behind the Army base," Quirk said, "across from Castle Hill Terminal."

We went into town on Boylston and turned right on Arlington. The store windows were full of red ribbon and spray-on snow. The streets were full of slush.

"Area C got a truck out there with a winch and hauled it out. It's a rental from Western Mass. There's a stiff in it."

"I.D. the stiff yet?" I said.

"No," Quirk said. "But there's a note for you."

Belson went under the expressway and up and through the South Station Tunnel with his siren whooping and his blue lights flashing. He slid off onto Atlantic Avenue and turned out Summer Street at the South Station.

The Boston Army Base is shabby, half used, dilapidated and full of nostalgia for most of us who processed through it on the way to wars someplace, quite some time ago. It had been the first stop on my long trip to Korea. At the end of the pier, there were three white cruisers with the blue stripe on the sides, a big tow truck with a crane arrangement on the back, the Fire Department rescue truck, and a couple of pickup trucks with diver's gear in the back. Belson flicked off the siren and lights and pulled in behind the rescue truck. Another nondescript municipal car pulled up behind us.

"Lupo," Belson said. "Medical Examiner."

We all got out and walked toward the red Chevette that sat on the hot top in a puddle of water. Water dripped from the open doors. The body was streaked with salt water, and in the front seat, still strapped with a safety belt, was a sodden dark mass of someone. Lupo, the assistant M.E., went briskly over and squatted on his haunches by the open side door and looked at the sodden someone. Quirk and I walked over and stood behind Lupo. Belson leaned on the car and began to look at the crime area, not looking for anything, just cataloguing.

Lupo straightened and spoke to Quirk.

"He's dead."

"I'm with you so far," Quirk said.

Lupo was a mild-looking man with a plain horsey face and prominent teeth. He had a pronounced widow's peak on his forehead and his hair was jet black though his face looked sixty-five. He wore a gabardine storm coat with a dark brown fur collar and lapels.

"Neck's broken," Lupo said. His upper teeth looked even and shiny as if they'd been capped. "Might have killed him, might have been dead when it got broken. He's pretty banged up."

"You want to look?" Quirk said to me.

"Oh, boy," I said.

I leaned in past Lupo and looked at the sodden thing. It had been Wilfred Pomeroy. His head lay on his shoulder at an odd angle. There was blood crusted in his nostrils. Some sort of sea sludge had clung to his cheek as the car was hauled out of the water. He was wearing a gray crew sweater and corduroy slacks that had probably been white, and a pair of cheap sneakers. His bare ankles were gray, the skin puckered a little by the seawater.

"Full rigor," Lupo was saying to Quirk.

I took in a long breath of cold sea air. It was mixed with the taste of gasoline slick, and garbage and the exhaust from the motors idling in the Area C prowl cars.

"Name's Wilfred Pomeroy," I said. "Was married to Jill Joyce once."

"Good how you knew him and we didn't," Quirk said.

I nodded. The wind off the water was hard, and in the twenty-degree air it felt arctic. Some seagulls who didn't appear to give a rat's ass about the wind or the temperature squalled and swooped around us, lighting on some of the pilings and then swooping off again almost as soon as they'd landed. Like most of the gulls on the east coast they were herring gulls, white and gray, with webbed feet and big wings. Their beaks were sharp and their eyes glittered as they rode the winds about us.

Quirk spoke to one of the uniformed cops.

"You talk to the security guard?"

"Yes, sir," the cop said. "He's over here. You want to see him?"

"What'd he tell you?"

"Says he was making his rounds, about four-thirty this morning. Says he makes them every hour and last time there wasn't nothing there, but at four-thirty he sees the tail end of this car sticking out of the water over the pier. So he calls us."

"Where was the envelope?" Quirk said.

"Watchman found it on top of one of the pilings there, near where the car went over. There was a brick on top of it."

"Gimme," Quirk said.

The young cop went to the squad car and returned with a manila envelope wrapped in some sort of clear plastic and taped along the seams. Quirk took it and looked at it and handed it to me. Through the plastic wrap I could see that it was addressed to me, care of the Boston Police Department.

"Open it," Quirk said.

I did. Inside was a page from a newspaper, the Berkshire *Argus*. The headline read, "Waymark Man Linked to TV Murder." There was an old picture of Pomeroy in his Navy uniform, and a story that quoted Waymark police chief Buford Phillips. It mentioned that Pomeroy had been married to the famous Jill Joyce and had recently been questioned by a Boston detective about the murder on the set of *Fifty Minutes*.

"Shit," I said.

Across the top of the tear sheet was scribbled, *Say good-bye to Jill for me.*

I handed the tear sheet to Quirk. He read it.

"A detective from Boston," he said.

"That goddamn Phillips," I said. "Couldn't wait to go blat to the papers."

"Tell me about this detective from Boston," Quirk said.

He carefully put the tear sheet back in the envelope and rewrapped it with the plastic wrap.

"Wanted to make sure it wouldn't get wet," I said.

"Suicides are sometimes very careful," Quirk said.

"Rojack told me about Pomeroy. He was Jill Joyce's first husband, maybe only. I don't know if they were divorced or not. He lived up in the Berkshires in Waymark."

"Waymark?" Quirk said.

"Out around Goshen," I said. "Ashfield."

"Sure," Quirk said.

"Hadn't seen her in twenty-five years, and carrying the torch the whole time."

"He drink?" Quirk said.

"Used to. Quit, he said, five years ago."

Quirk looked at the stiffening corpse. "Why bother?" he said.

I shrugged. "Then she shows up in Boston," I said. "Two hours away, on location, shooting this television series."

Two guys from the Medical Examiner's office eased Pomeroy's remains into a body bag and heaved it into the back of the wagon.

"It was too much," I said. "He started trying to see her. She didn't want him around. She didn't want some reformed drunk shitkicker from Waymark, Mass., turning out to be her husband, and the press hear of it. Guy was on welfare, hadn't heard from her since she dumped him."

"Wouldn't help her image," Quirk said.

"So she gets Rojack to get Randall to chase him off, which Randall does."

"And then you talk to Rojack and he tells you about Pomeroy and you go out to see him."

"Yeah."

"And you didn't tell us about him."

"Guy is about two-thirds of a person," I said. "Or he was. He's a sober alcoholic, hanging on barely, living in the woods with three dogs, trying to get over something that happened to him twenty-five years ago. He didn't kill Babe Loftus."

"You might wanta let us reach that conclusion on our own," Quirk said.

I shrugged. The body was in the back of the Examiner's wagon. The two technicians went around and got in front. Lupo walked past us toward his car.

"I'll be in touch," he said to Quirk.

"Anything says it isn't suicide?"

"Not yet," Lupo said.

Quirk nodded.

"I give you a lot of slack," he said, "because usually you end up on the right side of things, and sometimes you even help things. But don't think I won't rein you in if I need to."

"My mistake was talking to that goddamn shitkicker police chief," I said.

"You'd have been better talking to me," Quirk said.

"At least we agree on that," I said.

"How come he drove all the way here from Wayfar," Quirk said, "to take the jump?"

"Waymark," I said. "He wanted to be sure she'd hear about it. If he did it in Waymark it might make the Berkshire *Argus,* and who'd know? Who'd tell her? That's why he left the note for me too."

"And you can't tell her," Quirk said, "after all that trouble, because you don't know where she is."

"Yet," I said.

32

SUSAN had on glistening spandex tights and a green shiny leotard top and a white headband and white Avia workout shoes and she was charging up the stair climber like Teddy Roosevelt. I had on a white shirt and a leather jacket and I was leaning against one of the Kaiser Cam weight machines in her club watching her. When she exercised Susan didn't glow delicately. She sweated like a horse, and as she thundered up the Stair Master she blotted her face with a hand towel. I was admiring Susan's gluteus maximi as she climbed. She saw me in the mirror and said, "Are you staring at my butt?"

"Yes," I said.

"What do you think?" she said. I knew she was making a large effort to speak normally and not puff. She was a proud woman.

"I think it's the stuff dreams are made of, blue eyes."

"My eyes are black," Susan said.

"I know, but I can't do a good Bogart on 'black eyes.' "

"Some would say that was true of any color eyes," Susan said.

"Some have no ear," I said.

Susan was too out of wind to speak more, a fact which she concealed by shaking her head amusedly and pretending to concentrate harder on the stairs.

"You still working on the glutes?" I said.

"Un huh."

"No need," I said. "They get any better you'll have to have them licensed."

"You are just trying to get me to admit I can't talk and exercise," Susan said. "Go downstairs."

"You know the only other times I see you sweat like this?" I said.

"Yes," she said. "Go downstairs."

"Sure," I said.

An hour and a half later Susan was wearing a vibrant blue blouse and a black skirt and we were sitting across from each other at a table in Toscano Restaurant eating tortellini and drinking some white wine, for lunch.

"Did you hear anything from the police?" Susan said. "About Jill?"

"No," I said. "Not about Jill."

I broke off a piece of bread and ate it.

"Wilfred Pomeroy killed himself."

"The one Jill was married to?"

"Yeah. Came down to Boston, left a note for me, and drove off a pier."

"Why?"

"Press got hold of his story," I said. "He couldn't stand it, I guess. As if a magic lantern threw the nerves in patterns on a screen."

"Maybe," she said. "And maybe it was his chance

to make the *beau geste,* to die for her, rather than let his life be used against her."

"And a chance to say, simultaneously, *See how I loved you, see what you missed, see what you made me do.*"

"Suicide is often, *see what you made me do,*" Susan said. "It is often anger coupled with despair."

I nodded. Susan nibbled on one of the tortellini. She was the only person I knew who could eat one tortellini in several bites.

"Is tortellini better than sex?" she said.

"Not in your case," I said. "If you eat only one at a time of tortellini, are you eating a tortellenum?"

"You'll have to ask an Italian," Susan said. "I can barely conjugate *goyim.*"

We were quiet for a time. Concentrating on the food, sipping our wine. As always when I was with her, I could feel her across the table, the way one can feel heat, a tangible connection, silent, invisible, and realer than the pasta.

"Poor man," Susan said.

"Yeah."

"Will you find her, you think?"

"Yeah," I said.

Susan smiled at me and the heat thickened.

"Yes," she said, and leaned across the table and put her hand on top of mine, "you will."

33

AFTER lunch I dropped Susan at Harvard, where she taught a once-a-week seminar on analytic psychotherapy.

"You're going to stumble into the classroom reeking of white wine?" I said.

"I'll buy some Sen-Sen," Susan said.

"You consumed nearly an ounce," I said, "straight."

"A slave to Bacchus," she said. "Drive carefully."

She got out and I watched her walk away, until she was out of sight. "Hot damn," I said aloud, and pulled out into traffic.

I went through Harvard Square and down to the river, and across and onto the Mass. Pike. In about an hour and forty-five minutes I was in Waymark again. It took me a couple of tries but I found the road leading into Pomeroy's cabin. There had been snow here, that we hadn't gotten in eastern Mass., and I had to shift into four-wheel drive to get the Cherokee down the rutted road.

The cabin door was locked when I got there, and inside I heard the dogs bark. I knocked just to be proper and when no one answered but the dogs I backed off and kicked the door in. The dogs barked hysterically as the door splintered in, and then came boiling out past me into the yard. They stopped barking and began circling hurriedly until they each found the proper spot and relieved themselves, a lot. Inside the cabin there was a bowl on the floor half full of water, and another, larger bowl that was empty. I found a 25-pound sack of dry dog food and poured some into the bowl and took the rest out and put it in the back of the Cherokee. Finished with their business, the dogs hurried indoors and gathered at the food bowl. They went in sequence, one after another until all three were eating at once. While they ate I found some clothesline in the cabin and fashioned three leashes. When they were done I looped my leashes around their necks and took them to the car. They didn't leap in easily, like the dogs in station wagon commercials. They had to be boosted, one after the other, into the back seat. Once they were in I unlooped the rope and dropped it on the floor of the back seat, closed the back door, got in front and pulled out of there.

On the paved and plowed highway I shifted out of four-wheel drive and cruised down to police headquarters. The patrol car was parked outside. It looked like a cop car designed by Mr. Blackwell. I left the dogs in the Cherokee and went on in to see Phillips.

He was behind his desk, his cowboy boots up on the desk top, reading a copy of *Soldier of Fortune*. He looked up when I came in, and it took him a minute to place me.

"You went out and hassled him, didn't you?" I said.

Phillips was frowning, trying to remember who I was.

"Huh?" he said.

"Pomeroy. When I left you went back out there and made him tell you everything he told me, and then you couldn't keep it to yourself, you went to the *Argus* and blatted out everything you knew, and got your picture taken and your name spelled right, and ruined what was left of the poor bastard's life."

Phillips had figured out who I was, but he kept frowning.

"Hey, I got a right to conduct my own investigation," he said. "I'm the fucking law out here, remember?"

"Law, shit," I said. "You're a fat loudmouth in a jerkwater town playacting Wyatt Earp. And you cost an innocent man his life."

"You can't talk to me that way. Whose life?"

"Pomeroy killed himself this morning, in Boston. He had a copy of the Berkshire *Argus* story with him."

"Guy was always a loser," Phillips said.

"Guy loved too hard," I said. "Too much. Not wisely. You understand anything like that?"

"I told you, you can't come in here, talk to me like that, that tone of voice. I'll throw your ass in jail."

Phillips let his feet drop off the desk top and stood up. His hand was in the area of his holstered gun.

"You do that," I said. "You throw my ass in jail,

or go for the gun, or take a swing at me, anything you want."

I had moved closer to him, almost without volition, as if he were gravitational.

"Do something," I said. I could feel the tension across my back. "Go for the gun, take a swing, go for it."

Phillips' eyes rolled a little, side to side. There was a fine line of sweat on his upper lip. He looked at the phone. He looked at me. He looked past me at the door.

"Whyn't you just get out of here and leave me alone," he said. His voice was hoarse and shaky. "I didn't do nothing wrong."

We faced each other for another long, silent moment. I knew he wasn't going to do anything.

"I didn't do nothing wrong," he said again.

I nodded and turned and walked out. And left the door open behind me. That'd fix him.

34

"I KNOW people who might take one dog," Susan said. "But three? Mongrels?"

"I'm not breaking them up," I said.

We were in my living room and the dogs were around looking at us. The alpha dog was curled in the green leather chair; the other two were on the couch.

"Where did they sleep last night?" Susan said.

I shrugged.

Susan's eyes brightened.

"They slept with you," she said.

I shrugged again.

"You and the three doggies all together in bed. Tell me at least they slept on top of the quilt."

I shrugged.

"Hard as nails," Susan said.

"Well," I said. "I started them out in the kitchen, but then they started whimpering in the night . . ."

"Of course," Susan said, "and they got in there and you sleep with the window open, and it was cold . . ."

"You're the same way," I said.

Susan laughed. "Yes," she said. "I too think the bedroom's too cold."

"Dogs do not respect one's sleeping space much," I said.

"Did we sleep curled up on one small corner of the bed while the three pooches spread out luxuriously?" Susan said.

"I wanted them to feel at home," I said.

"We must be very clear on one thing. When I visit, we are not sleeping with three dogs."

"No," I said.

"And when we make love we are not going to be watched by three dogs."

"Of course not," I said. "Hawk says he knows some woman owns a farm in Bridgewater and is an animal rights activist."

"Don't tell her about my fur coat," Susan said.

"He thinks she'll take them."

Susan put the palm of her right hand flat on her chest and did a Jack E. Leonard impression. "I hope so," she said, "for your sake."

"You wouldn't like to take them over to your place today," I said. "I need to go to my office."

"I have meetings all day," she said. "It's why I'm here for breakfast."

"Oh yeah."

"I'm sure they'll love your office," Susan said.

And they did, for brief stretches. Every hour or so they felt the need to be walked down to the Public Garden. In between walks they sat, usually in a semicircle, and looked at me expectantly, with their mouths open and their tongues hanging out. All day.

Outside, Christmas was making its implacable approach. The dryness in the mouth of merchandising managers was intensifying, the exhaustion had become bone deep in the parents of small children, the television stations kept wishing me the best of the joyous season every station break, and the street gangs in Roxbury and Dorchester were shooting each other over insults to their manhood at the rate of about three a week. In the stores downtown people jostled each other; bundled uncomfortably in clothing against the cold, they were hot and angry in the crowded aisles where people sold silk show handkerchiefs and imported fragrances for the special person in your life. Liquor stores were doing a land-office business, and the courts were in double session trying to clear the calendar for the holiday break.

I got up and went to the old wood file cabinet behind the door and got out a bottle of Glenfiddich that Rachel Wallace had delivered to me last Christmas. It was still half full. I poured about two ounces in the water glass and went back to my desk. I sipped a little and let it vaporize in my mouth. Outside my window the dark winter afternoon had merged into the early darkness of a winter evening. I sipped another taste of the scotch. I raised my glass toward the dogs.

"Fa la la la la," I said.

I could feel the single-malt scotch inch into my veins. I sipped another sip. In my desk was a letter from Paul Giacomin in Aix-en-Provence in France. I took it out and read it again. Then I put it back into the envelope and put the envelope back in my desk drawer. I swiveled my chair so I could put my feet on the window sill and gaze out at the unoccupied air space where Linda Thomas had once worked. Beyond it was a building that looked like an old Philco radio. A Philip Johnson building, they said. I raised my glass to it.

"Way to go, Phil," I said. Lucky I hadn't been assigned to guard it. Probably lose it. *Was right here when I left it.* My glass was empty. I got up and got the bottle and poured another drink and went back and sat and stared out the dark window. The dogs stood when I stood, sat back down when I did.

The light fused up from the street the way it does in a city and softened into a pinkish glow at the top of the darkened buildings. Maybe she was dead. Maybe she wasn't. Maybe the pills and powders and booze and self-delusion and bullshit had busted her, and she had simply run and was running now.

I looked at the pinkish glow some more. I had nowhere I needed to be, nothing I needed to do. Susan was shopping. What if Jill had gone home? To her mother. To the hovel in the middle of the putrid hot field in the back alley of Esmeralda. I called Lipsky.

"Maybe she went to her mother's," I said.

"Esmeralda police checked," Lipsky said. "No sign of her. Just the old lady, or what's left of her."

"You thought of it," I said.

"Honest to God," Lipsky said and hung up.

I drank a little more scotch. I had a feeling I might drink a lot more scotch. One of the dogs got up and went to the corner and drank from the bowl of water I'd put down. He came back with water dripping from his muzzle and sat and resumed staring.

The phone rang. When I answered an accentless voice at the other end said, "This is Victor del Rio."

"Hey," I said. *"Qué pasa?"*

"She is here," del Rio said.

"In L.A.?" I said.

"Here, with me," del Rio said. "I think you better come out and get her."

35

I HAD my ticket. I was packed: clean shirt, extra blackjack. And I was having breakfast with Hawk and Susan, in the public atrium of the Charles Square complex in Cambridge.

"Jewish American Princesses," Susan was saying, "particularly those with advanced academic degrees, do not baby-sit dogs."

I looked at Hawk.

"That is even more true," he said, "of African American Princes."

The three mongrels, tethered by clothesline, sat in their pre-ordered circle, tongues lolling, eyes fixed on each morsel of croissant as it made its trip from paper plate to palate.

"Can you imagine them tearing around my place," Susan said, "with all the geegaws and froufrous I have in there, getting hair, yuk, on my white rug?"

I was silent, drinking my coffee carefully from the large paper cup, holding it in both hands. Hawk broke off a piece of croissant, divided it into three morsels and gave one each to the dogs. They took it delicately, in each case, from his fingers and stayed in place, eyes alert, after a quick swallow, and a fast muzzle lick, tongues once again lolling.

"Put 'em in a kennel," Hawk said. "Till my friend in Bridgewater gets back."

I looked at the three dogs. They gazed back at us, their eyes hazel with big dark pupils and full of more meaning than there probably was. They weren't young dogs, and there was a stillness in them, perhaps of change and strangeness, that had been in place since I got them.

"I don't think they should go in a kennel," Susan said. "They've had some pretty bad disruptions in the last few days already."

Hawk shrugged. He looked at the dogs again.

"Huey, Dewey, and Louie," he said.

We all sat in silence, drinking coffee, eating our croissants. A blond woman wearing exercise clothes under a fur coat passed us, carrying a tray with two muffins on it. The dogs all craned their heads over nearly backwards sniffing the muffins as they went by, and when the scent moved out of range they returned their stare to us.

"Well," Susan said, "I could come over to your place and stay with them at night. But during the day, I have patients."

I nodded. We both looked at Hawk.

Hawk looked at the dogs.

They stared back at him.

"What happens during the day?" Hawk said.

"They need to be walked."

"How often?"

"Three, four times," I said.

"Every day?"

"Yuh."

Hawk looked at me. He looked at Susan and then back at the dogs.

"Shit," he said.

"That's a part of it," I said.

"I meant shit, as in *oh shit!*" Hawk said.

"You and Susan can work it out in detail between you," I said. "My plane leaves in an hour."

Hawk was looking at me with a gaze that one less optimistic than I might interpret as hatred. I patted the dogs. Susan stood and we hugged and I kissed her. Hawk was still gazing at me. I put my hand out, palm up. He slapped it lightly.

"Thanks, bro," I said.

"Honkies suck," he said.

I took a cab to the airport. The plane took off on time, and I flew high above the fruited plain for six hours, cheered by the image of Hawk walking the three dogs.

36

DEL Rio had her in a hotel on Sunset in West Hollywood, a big one with a great view of the L.A. Basin. She was in one bedroom of a two-bedroom suite. The Indian in the Italian suit who had first taken me to see del Rio was in there, in the living room, reading the L.A. *Times* with his feet up on the coffee table. He had on a white cotton pullover today, and I could see the outline of a gun stuck in the waistband of his tight pocketless gray slacks. He glanced up once when Chollo brought me in, then went back to the paper.

"Vic in with her?" Chollo said.

The Indian nodded. Chollo nodded at one of the chairs.

"Sit," he said.

I sat. The room was large and square with the wall of picture windows facing south and the brownish haze above the basin, slightly below eye level, stretching to some higher ground in the distant south. To the left I could see the black towers of downtown poking up above the smog and to the right the coastline, fusing with the smog line in a sort of indiscriminate variation. The room itself was aggressively modern with bars of primary color painted on various portions of it and round-edged chrome structured furniture. The air conditioning was silent but effective. The room was nearly cold. Chollo leaned on the wall near one of the bedroom doors and gazed at nothing. His lips were pursed as if he were whistling silently to himself. His arms were folded comfortably across his chest. He was wearing a blue blazer over a white polo shirt. The collar of the shirt was turned up. I crossed one leg over the other and watched my toe bob. When I got bored I could cross my legs the other way.

I stared at the view.

After about ten minutes del Rio came out of the bedroom and closed the door behind him. He looked at me and nodded once. Then he looked at the Indian.

"Bobby, wait outside."

The Indian got up, folded the newspaper over, and went out of the hotel suite. He closed the door behind him. Del Rio went to the bar in one corner of the room. There were three stools at the bar. He sat on one of them. Chollo peeled off the wall and went past him and behind the bar. He mixed a tall scotch and soda, added ice, and handed it to del Rio. Del Rio looked at me and gestured with the glass.

"Sure," I said. "Same thing. Lots of ice."

Chollo made me a drink, and then poured out a short one and tossed it off himself, put the glass back on the bar, leaned back against the mirrored wall behind the bar, and waited. Del Rio sampled his drink, smiled.

"It's blended," he said.

"Want I should call down for a single malt?" Chollo said.

Del Rio shook his head. "Won't be here that long, I hope."

I tasted my drink. I couldn't tell, not with the soda and ice. Del Rio took another sip.

"Nice to see you again, Spenser."

"Sure," I said. "When do I see Jill?"

"Pretty soon. I think we better talk first."

I waited. Chollo refolded his arms behind the bar and his gaze fixed on something in the middle distance. Del Rio was in black today, a black silk suit, double breasted, with a white silk shirt, and a narrow black scarf at the open neck. He wore black cowboy boots with silver inlays. Del Rio tasted his drink again.

"She showed up here yesterday morning in a state. Barely functional. She doesn't know where I live, but she came to one of the, ah, offices I use in East L.A. and told the guy there that she had to see me."

"Guy know who she was?" I said.

"Yes. But he is discreet. So he called the house and Bobby Horse went down and got her and brought her here. I keep a suite here, anyhow."

"Of course," I said. "Anyone would."

"Chollo and I met her here, and she and I talked for a long while."

"She offer to ball you?" I said.

"Of course," del Rio said.

"And you declined," I said.

"Perhaps that is not your business," del Rio said.

"Perhaps you called me," I said.

Del Rio nodded. "She said that I was the only one who could help her. That no one else would help her and that *He* was going to get her.

"I asked her who *He* was. She said she didn't know. I asked her how she knew *He* was trying to get her. She said *He*'d called her again, the night she took off."

"You know when that was?"

"Yes. It made the papers. Especially here," del Rio said. "This is a company town." He sipped his scotch, looking at the glass. "Times when there's nothing better," he said. I nodded and rattled the ice around in my glass a little and took a small sip.

"I asked her what *He* said to her. She said *He* said awful things."

"That's our Jill," I said. "Full of hard information."

"She said you wouldn't protect her, that some guy named Hawk wouldn't protect her, that the studio didn't give a shit, and that I was all she had left. She said I had to help her."

"What are you supposed to do?" I said.

"Make *Him* leave her alone."

"But she doesn't know who *Him* is."

"This is true," del Rio said.

"So what do you want me to do?" I said.

"Get her the fuck out of here," del Rio said. "I don't want her around."

"Has she threatened to reveal all?" I said.

"She knows better," del Rio said. "But she's such a mess that I'm afraid she may cause trouble without meaning to, and I don't want to have to dump her to prevent it."

"What a softie," I said.

"Don't make that mistake," del Rio said. "You want to talk with her?"

"In a minute," I said. "What do you think?"

"About her?"

"Yeah."

"I think she needs a shrink."

I nodded. "How about the mysterious *He*?"

"I think it's in her head," del Rio said.

"Who killed Babe Loftus?" I said.

Del Rio shrugged, turned his palms up. "Hey, I'm a simple Mexican," he said. "That's your line of work."

"And I'm doing it grand," I said.

"Grand," del Rio said.

"What about the harassment?" I said. "The hanged doll—that stuff?"

"I think she did it herself," del Rio said. "She's trying to get people's attention."

"It's working," I said.

A dark cloud had drifted up from the basin and some big raindrops splattered occasionally on the picture window. We all sat in silence.

"She drinking?" I said.

"If she cut back, she'd be drinking," del Rio said. "You want a refill?"

I shook my head.

"Let's talk with her," I said.

Del Rio nodded, and Chollo went around the bar and opened the door to the bedroom. He said something I couldn't hear and, in a moment, Jill came out. You could see that she'd been crying. Her eyes were puffy. The eyeliner was gone, or most of it was. Her nose was red. Her hair was uncombed and looked as if she'd been running her fingers through it. She was soused to the lip line and it showed in the unsteadiness of her walk.

"Well, damn," she said when she saw me. "The big dick from Boston." She went to the bar and put her glass out on it. Chollo went around without comment and fixed her a new drink, scotch, water, ice. She stopped his hand after he'd added only a splash of water.

"What you doing out here, Big Dick?"

Behind the bar Chollo had no expression. Del Rio put his hands behind his head and leaned back in his chair as if to give me my turn, see what I could do.

"Why'd you run off?" I said.

"He called."

"The night you left?"

"Yes."

"And you don't know who he is?"

"No."

"What'd he say?"

She shook her head.

"Did he threaten you?"

She nodded.

"What did he threaten you with?"

She shook her head again.

"Why won't you say?"

She drank most of her drink before she answered.

"Don't be so fucking nosy," she said.

"How in hell am I going to help you if I don't know what I'm trying to help you with?"

"Maybe if you'd get off your ass and catch him," she said, "and put him away where he belongs . . . that might help, you know?"

She finished her drink, held the glass out, and Chollo replenished it. Del Rio's dark compassionless eyes watched her carefully.

"Anything else happen that night?" I said.

She shrugged.

"Hawk make a pass at you?"

"How'd you know?" she said. She got a crafty look on her face.

"He said there was some talk of, ah, hanky-panky, but it didn't, if you'll pardon the expression, come to anything."

"You bet your ass," she said. "I'm not fucking some coon."

"So you turned him down," I said.

"Sure, limp dick motherfucker. He's a tighter ass than you."

"And that's why you turned him down."

"You bet your buns. Lotta men give up a year of

their life to fuck me. But you goddamned pansies." She tossed her chin at del Rio. "Him too."

"Yes," I said. "I understand you brushed him off tonight too."

She nodded righteously and drank more scotch.

"When *He* called, the bad guy, the man who threatened you, how did he get through?" I said.

"Huh?"

"How did he reach you?"

"He just called up," she said. "I answered the phone."

"This was after Hawk left you," I said. "After eleven?"

"Sure."

"Are you telling me that anyone, without even giving a name, could call up the Charles Hotel at, say, eleven-thirty at night and be put right through to your room, no questions asked?"

The crafty look got a little fogged over; her brows furrowed. She wasn't a deep thinker sober, and she was a long distance past sober. She opened her mouth once, and closed it again. She looked at del Rio. She drank some scotch. I waited.

"Leave me alone," she said.

"Jill," I said, "the only way anyone can call your room is to be on a call list, and identify themselves. You know that. I know that. I'm on the list. Otherwise half the city of Boston would call you up every day. You're a star."

"You're goddamned right I am," Jill said. "And you better, goddamn it, start treating me like one."

Her breath seemed short. Her face was reddening. "Somebody better," she said.

She let her head drop and took hold of her drink with both hands and then her shoulders sagged forward.

"Somebody better," she said again and started to cry. The crying was hysterical and had the promise of duration. I looked at del Rio. He looked at me. Chollo looked at whatever he looked at. We waited. After a while she stopped sobbing long enough to get a cigarette going and sip some scotch.

"Why won't anyone take care of me," she said in a gasping voice and started to cry again. Through the picture window I could see that the dark cloud had moved directly over us. The occasional raindrops that had spattered on the window intensified. They came now in a steady rattle.

Del Rio said, "Would you like to see your mother, Jill?" There was no kindness in his voice, but no cruelty either.

"God, no," Jill said, still crying, her face buried in her hands, the cigarette drifting smoke from her right hand.

"Maybe your father," I said. "Would you like to talk with your father?"

She sat suddenly upright. "My father's dead," she said and continued to cry, sitting up, facing us, occasionally swigging in a gulp of scotch or dragging in a lungful of smoke, between sobs. I turned that over in my mind a little.

"Your father's not dead, Jill. He's here in Los Angeles."

"He's dead," she said.

"I've talked with him," I said. "Only a week or so ago."

"He's dead," she screamed at me. "Goddamn it, my father is dead. He died when I was little and he left me with my mother."

She drank off the rest of her drink as the echoes of her scream were rattling around the hotel room, and then she pitched suddenly forward and passed out, facedown on the floor. I reached down and took the burning cigarette from her hand and put it out in an ashtray. Chollo came around the bar, and he and I picked her up and carried her into the bedroom. We put her on her back, on her bed. I put the spread over her and we left her there and came back out into the living room.

"Lushes," Chollo said. "Lushes are crazy."

Del Rio was where we had left him, sitting still with his hands clasped behind his head.

"Know anything about her father?" I said.

"She told me he left when she was a kid. Coulda meant he died. I took it to mean he just left," del Rio said. "Who's this guy you talked to?"

"Guy named Bill Zabriskie, her agent put me onto him."

"She sure threw a wingding when you said he was alive," del Rio said.

"Yeah," I said. "You got someone to run an errand?"

Del Rio nodded.

"Chollo," he said, "tell Bobby Horse to come in here."

37

WHEN Jill woke up it was late, nearly midnight. She must have felt like someone's leftover meal when she stumbled out of the bedroom. Chollo had black coffee and a carafe of orange juice sent up. Jill drank both and smoked a cigarette before she said a word. Her face was pale, and her hair was matted from sleeping on it, and there was a wrinkle grooved into her cheek by a fold in the pillow cover.

"Got some brandy?" she said. Chollo came around the bar and poured some into her coffee. She sipped it.

"Ahh," she said. "Hair of the dog that bit you."

Del Rio was still there, and so was I. Chollo was in place behind the bar.

"Want something to eat?" del Rio said in his clear voice.

Jill shivered.

"God, no," she said. She looked at her reflection in the now-dark window. "Jesus," she said. "Am I a mess."

"Somebody here to see you," I said.

"Like this?" Jill said. Her hand shook as she lifted her coffee cup, and she slopped a little of the brandy-laced coffee onto her lap. She brushed absently at it with her free hand.

"Be all right," I said. "You look fine."

Del Rio raised his voice only slightly.

"Bobby Horse," he said.

The Indian opened the door to the other bedroom and came out with Bill Zabriskie. Zabriskie had on the same woven sandals as I'd seen him in. He also had on tan polyester pants and a white Western-style shirt, hanging loose, with one of those little strings held by a silver clasp at the neck.

He squinted a little, as if the light were too bright, and then went and sat carefully down on the edge of one of the armchairs. He looked slowly at Jill without reaction. Jill looked at him the same way.

"Who's this?" she said.

"What's your name?" I said to him.

"William Zabriskie."

"You ever married to a woman named Vera Zabriskie?" I said.

Jill had frozen in her chair, the half-drunk coffee in her right hand. There was stiffness in the outline of her shoulders.

"Sure," Zabriskie said. He looked at his watch, which he wore on his right wrist. It was a cheap black plastic one, the kind where the wristband is built into the watch, and if you want, you can set lap times in the stopwatch mode. "Are you police?"

"You have a daughter?" I said.

"Yes. A famous TV star, her name is Jill Joyce now."

"What was her name?"

"Jillian. Jillian Zabriskie," he said. "Why do you keep asking me these things?"

Jill dropped the coffee cup. It broke on the floor and coffee stained the rug. No one paid any attention.

"You see her in the room anywhere?" I said.

Zabriskie looked at Jill, as if he hadn't noticed her before. He squinted even though the light was good.

"That looks like her."

I turned to Jill. She had shrunk back into her chair, her knees drawn up toward her chest, her arms hugging her elbows in against her. Her skin seemed drawn tight over the bones of her face. Her breath rasped in and out as if her windpipe had rusted.

"It's *Him,"* she gasped. Her voice was very hoarse. "You're dead. You have to be dead."

Zabriskie looked puzzled.

"I'm not dead," he said.

Jill shrank deeper in on herself.

"Don't," she said. "Don't." She looked at me. "Don't let him," she said. "I don't want to." Her voice got a sing-song in it, and the hoarseness faded and it sounded young. "I don't want to. I don't want you to do that to me. I don't like it. Please, Daddy, please. Please." She began to cry again. "Please."

Zabriskie stared at her blankly.

"Why did you never give me money?" he said. "You are my daughter and you are rich and you never give me money."

Jill was now in a ball, as tightly coiled in on herself

as she could get. She wasn't crying so much as whimpering, in on herself, like a small child, entirely alone, in terrible trouble. I went over and put my hand on her shoulder and she shrank, if possible, a bit tighter, and then tentatively put up one hand and placed it on mine. Everyone was quiet; the only sound was of Jill's small whimper.

The Indian said, "Jesus."

Zabriskie seemed unmoved, in fact he seemed unaware of Jill's response.

Jill raised her eyes toward me. "It's *Him,"* she said. "*He's* the one."

I nodded and squeezed her shoulder a little.

"You need money," I said to Zabriskie.

"Twenty-five years I worked there, and they let me go, when I got old."

"Where'd you work?"

"Weldon Oil, night security."

"Carry a gun?"

"Certainly."

I nodded.

"What'd Jill do when you asked her for money?"

"Never a chance to ask. Miss Movie Star wouldn't see me."

"You write her?"

"Yes."

"Go to see her agent?"

"Yes. She's rich. Yet she won't give her own father anything?"

I nodded again.

"Go to Boston to try and see her?"

"Went right to the set. Sent her a note. She never answered it."

"Tough," I said, "to be that desperate and that close."

"Miss Movie Star," he said.

"Maybe when she dies you'll collect," I said. "There don't seem to be a lot of heirs."

"At my age?" he said.

"Oh," I said. "Right."

"You fly to Boston?" I said.

"Bus," he said. As if the idea that he could afford to fly was as insane as suggesting he could fly there by flapping his arms.

"Long ride?"

"Three days," he said.

"Pack the gun in your luggage or carry it on?"

"Packed . . . what gun?" His empty eyes got smaller. "Why you asking me this?"

"No reason," I shrugged. "Just knew you'd brought a three fifty-seven with you and wondered if it was a problem getting it cross country."

"No," he said.

I could feel a great sadness settling in on me.

"You left-handed?" I said.

His eyes were very beady now, shrunk to suspicious points of hostility. I could feel Jill's hand press down on mine. She had stopped whimpering. Chollo behind the bar, the Indian, del Rio, all were motionless, some kind of frozen tapestry, silent witness to something awful being dragged into the light.

"What about it," he said.

"Nothing, just noticed you wore your watch on the right wrist, and I wondered. Once a detective, always a detective." I smiled my big friendly smile, old Pop Spenser, just a chatty guy, making small talk with an old man. How charming.

"I got a license for that gun," Zabriskie said. He was in trouble and dimly he knew it. He should have shut up, but the really stupid ones don't.

"It's a three fifty-seven magnum, right?"

"So what?"

"Colt?"

"Smith & Wesson."

"How about that," I said. "Made right out in Springfield, probably, practically next to Boston. Like bringing your gun home."

"I got a license."

"You bring it with you to kill your daughter?" I said.

"I didn't kill nobody," Zabriskie said.

"You killed Babe Loftus," I said. "By mistake."

The room crackled with silence. Nobody breathed. The rain had stopped long ago, and the sky had cleared, and below us in the basin the lights of Los Angeles gleamed like the promise of a thousand eyes. Jill's fingernails dug into my hand.

"You thought it was Jill," I said. "It had been so long."

The old man stood up.

"I'm going out of here now," he said.

Bobby Horse moved silently in front of the exit

door. Zabriskie stopped and turned and looked slowly around the room.

"You read about the harassment, and the bodyguard, and all. You figured people would assume her death was linked to whoever had been bothering her. You could shoot her and go back to L.A. and sit tight and in a while you'd inherit her money."

There was no expression on Zabriskie's face. He seemed solely interested in whether there was another exit.

"I'll bet," I said, "when the cops match up the bullet they took out of Babe with the test bullet they fire from your gun, it'll match."

The old man decided that there wasn't another exit. He looked down at Jill.

"You're an unloving and unnatural daughter," he said. "If you had given me some money . . ."

He put his left hand almost tiredly under his loose shirt and came out with the .357. Behind the bar Chollo didn't seem to move, except suddenly there was a gun in his hand, and it fired, and Zabriskie slammed backwards over the coffee table and bounced against the wall and slid slowly to the floor. By the time he hit the floor Chollo's gun was out of sight again. Jill, in her tight coil, turned her face against the chair and moaned.

"Quick," I said to Chollo. He smiled modestly.

Del Rio said, "Can you get her out of here and back to Boston?"

"Yeah," I said.

"Do you need money?"

"No. How about this, can you clean this up?" I said.

"I own the hotel," del Rio said. He smiled slightly. "Among other things."

I bent and edged my arms under her and picked Jill up from her chair. She put her arms around my neck and placed her face against my shoulder.

"Bobby Horse will drive you," del Rio said. "She's going to need a lot of attention. I want you to give it to her. On the other coast. You need money, call me."

"I won't need money," I said.

The Indian opened the door and I went through carrying Jill.

Behind me del Rio said, "Adios."

I paused and half turned and looked back at him and the still motionless Chollo.

"Si," I said.

38

I TOOK Jill up to Maine, to a cabin on a lake that I'd built with Paul Giacomin nine years before. The cabin belonged to Susan, but she let me use it. We got there on a Thursday, driving straight from the airport, and on Saturday morning while I was making breakfast Jill still hadn't spoken.

The snow was a foot deep in the woods, and the other cabins were empty. Nothing moved but squirrels and the winter birds that hopped along the snow crust and seemed impervious to cold. I kept a fire going in the big central fireplace, and read some books, and did push-ups and sit-ups. I would have run along the plowed highway, but I didn't want to leave Jill.

Jill was silent. She sat where I put her, she slept a lot, she ate some of what I gave her. She smoked and had coffee and in the evening would drink some. But she didn't drink a lot, and she spoke not at all. Much of the time she simply sat and looked at things I didn't see and seemed very far away inside.

I ate some turkey hash with corn bread, and two cups of coffee. Jill had some coffee and three cigarettes. It didn't seem too healthy to me, but I figured this might not be the time for rigorous retraining.

"I came up here, about nine years ago," I said, "with a kid named Paul Giacomin."

It was not clear, when I talked to her, if Jill heard me, though when I offered her coffee she held out her cup.

"Kid was a mess," I said. "Center of a custody dispute in a messy divorce. It wasn't that each parent wanted him. It was that neither parent wanted the other to have him."

I put a dab of cranberry catsup on my second helping of hash.

"We built this place, he and I. I taught him to carpenter, and to work out, read poetry. Susan got him some psychotherapy. Kid's a professional dancer now, he's in Aix-en-Provence, in France, performing and giving master's classes at some dance festival."

Jill had no reaction. I ate my hash. While I was cleaning up the breakfast dishes, the phone rang. It was Sandy Salzman.

"Studio's up my ass," Salzman said. "Network is talking cancellation. Where the fuck is she?"

"She's with me," I said.

"I know that, when the hell does she reappear?"

"Later," I said.

"I've got to talk with her," Sandy said. "Put her on the phone."

"No."

"Dammit, I've got to talk with her. I'm coming up."

"I won't let you see her," I said.

"For crissake, Spenser, you work for me."

"You can't see her," I said.

"Somebody from the studio, Riggs, somebody from business affairs?"

"Nobody," I said.

"Dammit, you can't stop me."

"Yes, I can."

"I'll bring some people."

"Better bring a lot," I said.

"Spenser, I've got authorization, from Michael Maschio himself, to terminate your services as of this moment."

"No," I said. "You don't see her. Her agent doesn't see her. Michael Maschio doesn't see her. Captain Kangaroo doesn't see her. Just me, I see her. And Susan Silverman. Nobody else until she's ready."

"Spenser, goddammit, you got no right . . ."

I hung up. In fifteen minutes I had a similar conversation with Jill's agent, who must have been calling before sunrise, West Coast time. At 9:45 I talked on the phone with Martin Quirk.

"We got the gun killed Loftus," he said without preamble when I answered the phone. "Registered to a guy named William Zabriskie. LAPD found him in the trunk of a stolen car parked in the lot of Bullocks Department Store on Wilshire Boulevard. Gun was on him. Been shot once through the heart."

"How'd they come to check with you?" I said.

"Anonymous tip," Quirk said.

"Got a motive?"

"No," Quirk said. "Why I'm calling you. Ever hear of this guy?"

"He's Jill Joyce's father," I said.

"The hell he is," Quirk said.

I was silent.

"And?" Quirk said.

"And I don't know what else, yet. I need a little time."

"I don't have any to give you," Quirk said. "I got lawyers from Zenith Meridien and the TV network and the governor's office and the Jill Joyce fan club camped outside my office. The D.A. wants my badge."

"Marty," I said, "he molested her as a child. She saw him killed."

The silence on the line was broken only by the faint crackle of the system.

"You got her up there with you?"

"Yeah."

"What kind of shape she in?"

"The worst," I said.

"Susan seen her?"

"Not yet."

More crackle on the line. Behind me Jill was watching the fire move among the logs.

"You can't keep her up there forever," Quirk said.

"I know."

"What are you going to do?"

"I don't know," I said. "I don't have a long-range plan. Right now I'm figuring out lunch."

"How long you need?"

"I don't know."

"You know how Zabriskie got killed?" Quirk said.

"Yes."

"You planning on sharing that with me?"

"Only off the record."

"Gee, I love being a homicide cop," Quirk said. "Get to ask people lots of questions and they have no answer."

"It's L.A.'s problem," I said.

"True," Quirk said.

Again we were silent, listening to the murmur of the phone system.

"I'll do what I can," Quirk said.

"Me too," I said.

We hung up.

Susan Silverman showed up at noon. She came in along the driveway too fast, like she always did, in her white sports car, only this time there were three mongrel dogs in it with her. They came out as she held the door for them, gingerly, sniffing carefully, the two junior dogs watching the alpha dog. After a moment of sniffing, they apparently established it as appropriate territory because they began to tear around, noses to the ground, investigating squirrel scent and bird tracks. Susan had brought with her a trunkful of groceries, and she was starting to unload them when I came out of the house.

"Time for that in a moment," I said and put my arms around her. She smelled of lilacs and milled soap and fresh air. She hugged me and we kissed and then we carried in the bags.

Susan smiled at Jill when she went in, and said, "Hi." Jill gazed at her without reaction. We went to the kitchen end of the cabin to put the groceries away.

"She talk yet?" Susan said.

"No."

"What's she been doing?"

I told her. Susan nodded.

"What do I do with her," I said.

"You can't help her," Susan said. "If you're right about her life she needs more than you can ever give her."

"I know."

"But you may be able to help get her to a point where she can be helped," Susan said.

"By giving her time?"

"Yes, and space, and quiet. Try to get her healthy. Eat more, drink less, some exercise. But don't push it. All of her addictions are probably symptoms, not causes, and will yield better to treatment when the source of her anguish is dealt with."

"Thanks, doctor," I said. "Care to shtup me?"

"How could I resist, you glib devil, you?"

"Can you wait until evening?"

"Anxiously," Susan said.

I had left the door ajar for the dogs, and now they nosed it open and came in, sniffing vigorously around the cabin, their eyes bright from their return to the woods. One of them sniffed at Jill as she sat there, and she turned and bent down toward it. It licked her face and she reached out suddenly and began to pat it. Susan nudged me and nodded, but I'd seen it already.

The other two dogs joined the first one and Jill took turns patting them. One of them reared on his hind legs and laid his forepaws in her lap and licked her face again. Jill put her arms around him and hugged him, her face against the side of his muzzle. Tears moved on her face. The dog looked a little anxious as she rocked sideways holding him in her arms, but then he discovered the salty tears and lapped them industriously, making no attempt to escape.

39

By the time Susan left on Sunday night, Jill was talking. She wasn't saying much. But she said *yes,* and *no.* As in:

"Would you like more coffee?"

"Yes."

"And would you like to take a walk?"

"No."

On Monday morning a reporter from the *Herald* showed up and I was forced to threaten him. I got phone calls from the *Globe* and all three network affiliates in Boston. I told each that I would shoot anyone I saw.

A half hour later I got a call from Rojack.

"I want to know how Jill is," he said.

"She's resting comfortably," I said.

"I'd like a bit more than that," he said.

"I don't blame you," I said. "How'd you get this number?"

"I know a lot of people," Rojack said. "Some of them are important."

"Nice for you," I said.

"I know you don't hold me in high regard, Spenser, but I care about Jill. I have the right to know how she is."

"Un huh," I said.

"You have no right to interfere. I want to see her."

"No."

"I love her, dammit, do you understand that?"

"Not in this case," I said. "You can't see her. Later, maybe."

"I'm afraid I must insist."

"Sure," I said. "That'll turn me inside out."

"If I can get the number, I can get the location," Rojack said. "Perhaps Randall and I will pay you a visit."

"Perhaps I will stick Randall in the lake," I said.

"Whatever you may think, Spenser, I love that woman. I want to help her."

"The way you help her now is to leave her alone."

"You won't change your mind?"

"No one sees her," I said.

"We'll be up. You were lucky with Randall the first time."

"I was kind the first time," I said. "This time he'll get hurt."

I heard the phone click. I hung up and looked at Jill sitting by the window in a straight chair looking at the lake, where the three dogs were busy sniffing out something. I picked up the phone and called Henry Cimoli and asked for Hawk. He was there.

"Remember I told you about a guy named Stanley Rojack?"

"Un huh."

"Walks around with a big geek named Randall, thinks he's tougher than Oliver North."

"Wow," Hawk said.

"They say they're going to come up here and bother us," I said.

Jill continued to watch the dogs through the window. If the name registered it didn't affect her.

"You want me to drive out and tell them not to?" Hawk said.

"Yeah," I said, and gave him the address. "Randall does karate," I said.

"Good," Hawk said. "It's fun to watch."

I hung up.

"That takes care of that," I said to Jill.

She made no response.

Jill spent a lot of time with the dogs. She got dressed for the first time, on Monday, wearing some clothes that Susan had bought her, and sat on the floor trying to get the dogs to take turns retrieving a ball. She did this in so soft a voice that I didn't know what she was saying, and when she spoke to the dogs she leaned very close and whispered in their ears. She ate some potato and leek soup for lunch with a homemade biscuit, and after lunch when I suggested a walk she said, "Can we take the dogs?"

"Sure."

And so we did. It was clear and sunny and maybe thirty-five degrees when we went out. Jill had on a red down-filled parka, and I wore my leather jacket. I had my gun on in case one of the squirrels got aggressive, and the three dogs raced out ahead of us, crisscrossing as we went, snuffling the ground and occasionally treeing one of the squirrels. When they did they'd moil silently around the base of the tree, leaping sometimes at the branch twenty feet above where the squirrel perched. *Hound's reach must exceed its grasp.*

We were on an old logging road, where the sun had caused faster snow melt than under the trees, and the melting had caused a sag in the snow cover that defined our way. The snow was only a few inches deep here and packed harder by the melt and refreeze cycle. We didn't say anything as we crunched along. Ahead the dogs began to bark frantically and dashed off to the west of the road. When we reached the place where they'd left the road I could see rabbit tracks, the neat front paw marks, the long slur of the back feet. With the dogs out of sight Jill looked anxiously after them.

"They'll be back," I said.

Jill nodded, but still she stared off in the direction of the dogs. In another minute the dogs reappeared, tongues lolling, bearing themselves proudly, as if they'd actually caught the rabbit. I could hear Jill's breath ease out in relief.

The road wound deeper into the woods, and where the trees had shaded it the snow was deeper and the going harder. Jill was beginning to puff, and I slowed my pace for her. She was slipping a little in the deeper snow, and I put my hand out. She took it. We walked on, holding hands. The dogs found a blue jay working on a pinecone and drove him up into the white pine tree behind him. One of them ran about for a while with the pinecone in his mouth. Finally he dropped it. The other dogs sniffed at it in turn but left it behind them as they ranged off in search of better. We were deep in the woods now, and there was no more trail. Jill held on to my hand as we went, and we crunched through the deeper snow in the evergreen woods. It was harder going, in deep; but she seemed to want to keep going. She was breathing hard and hanging on to me even harder when we broke from the woods and saw the lake again. It was frozen and snow covered, and there were the tracks of animals across it. We turned and walked along the margin of the lake. Here the sun had burned away the snow so that rocks showed and occasionally patches of earth with the grass dead and pale in the winter sunlight. The walking was easier. Ahead we could see the cabin. We had come in a slow loop back nearly to where we'd begun. The dogs saw the cabin and headed for it, running full out, heads extended, bodies bunching and flattening. They were milling at the front door when we got there and all three dashed for the water bowl and drank when I opened the door.

The fire was down and I added wood. There was electric heat in the place. The fireplace was more for show. But when it was going it warmed the room, and I turned the heat off. Jill took off her parka and hung it on the back of her chair and went and sat at the table and rested her chin on her elbows.

"I want a drink," she said.

I mixed two, and brought them to the table and

put one down in front of her. Then I sat at the table across from her.

"Here's looking at you, kid," I said. I sounded exactly like Humphrey Bogart. Jill drank a little and so did I. The new wood on the fire had blazed up and the flames frolicked in the fireplace. The afternoon light came at a low slant through the windows.

"Tonight," I said, "I'm going to grill chicken over the fire and serve it with succotash and hot biscuits with honey."

Jill nodded.

"Maybe some coleslaw. Do you like coleslaw? I make it without mayo."

Jill nodded again. The flames calmed a little as the logs settled in slightly on each other. The dogs were in their semicircle again, looking at us, waiting for dinner. I stood.

"Dogs are hungry," I said.

"I'll feed them," Jill said. And stood and went to the kitchen. She poured too much dry food into each of the three bowls and put them down and the dogs dug in. Then she came and sat down again and sipped her light scotch and soda and watched them eat. When she finished she held the glass out to me and I went and made her another light one. The dogs finished eating and settled in on the sofa, overlapping each other in ways that no human would find comfortable. The dogs seemed not to mind at all. In a minute they were asleep. Jill watched them.

"Have you ever wanted to go to bed with me?" Jill said.

"Every time I see you," I said.

"Why haven't you?"

"In love with someone else. We don't sleep around."

"She's a shrink," Jill said.

I nodded.

"Can she help me too?" Jill said.

"Yes," I said.

Jill was silent, thinking about this. She watched the dogs sleep while she thought. One of them shifted in his sleep and licked his muzzle with one slow sweep of his tongue.

"Why do you take care of me?" Jill said.

"No one else."

She thought about this for a while too. She drank her drink, but not as if she had to get it in quick. She nodded to herself.

"Do you like me?" she said.

"Yes," I said. "And it hasn't been easy."

Again she was quiet. The boss dog turned in his sleep and wriggled himself up on his back and slept that way, with all four paws in the air, legs flexed at the wrist, or whatever dogs called it, the paws hanging limp. The logs in the fireplace made a kind of sigh as they settled further, blending downward into the red mass of the coals.

"*He's* gone, isn't he," Jill said.

"Yes."

"You made him stop, didn't you?"

"He won't frighten you anymore," I said.

She took another swallow of her drink. She studied the dogs. The afternoon was gone from the window and the night had arrived. The cabin was dark except for the firelight.

"He will frighten me forever," Jill said.

"Maybe not," I said.

If you enjoyed

STARDUST

then don't miss Robert B. Parker's exciting sequel to the all-time mystery classic, THE BIG SLEEP . . .

Perchance to Dream

At last—Raymond Chandler's unfinished masterpiece featuring detective Phillip Marlowe—now completed by today's hottest mystery writer.

AVAILABLE IN HARDCOVER FROM G.P. PUTNAM'S SONS.

Here is a sample of this thrilling new work . . .

The gentle-eyed, horsefaced maid let me into the long gray and white upstairs sitting room with the ivory drapes tumbled extravagantly on the floor and the white carpet from wall to wall. A screen star's boudoir, a place of charm and seduction, artificial as a wooden leg. It was empty at the moment. The door closed behind me with the unnatural softness of a hospital door. A breakfast table on wheels stood by the chaise longue. Its silver glittered. There were cigarette ashes in the coffee cup. I sat down and waited. It seemed a long time before the door opened again and Vivian came in. She was in oyster-white lounging pajamas trimmed with white fur, cut as flowingly as a summer sea frothing on the beach of some small and exclusive island.

She went past me in long smooth strides and sat down on the edge of the chaise longue. There was a cigarette in her lips at the corner of her mouth. Her nails were copper red from quick to tip, without halfmoons.

"So you're just a brute after all," she said quietly,

staring at me. "An utter callous brute. You killed a man last night. Never mind how I heard it. I heard it. And now you have to come out here and frighten my kid sister into a fit."

I didn't say a word. She began to fidget. She moved over to a slipper chair, put her head back against a white cushion that lay along the back of the chair against the wall. She blew pale gray smoke upward and watched it float toward the ceiling and come apart in wisps that were for a little while distinguishable from the air and then melted and were nothing. Then very slowly she lowered her eyes and gave me a cool hard glance.

"I don't understand you," she said. "I'm thankful as hell one of us kept his head the night before last. It's bad enough to have a bootlegger in my past. Why don't you for Christ's sake say something?"

"How is she?"

"Oh, she's all right, I suppose. Fast asleep. She always goes to sleep. What did you do to her?"

"Not a thing. I came out of the house after seeing your father and she was out in front. She had been throwing darts at a target on a tree. I went down to speak to her because I had something that belonged to her. A little revolver Owen Taylor gave her once. She took it over to Brody's place the other evening, the evening he was killed. I had to take it away from her there. I didn't mention it, so perhaps you didn't know it."

The black Sternwood eyes got large and empty. It was her turn not to say anything.

"She was pleased to get her little gun back and she wanted me to teach her how to shoot and she wanted to show me the old oil wells down the hill where your family made some of its money. So we went down there and the place was pretty creepy, all rusted metal and old wood and silent wells and greasy scummy sumps. Maybe that upset her. I guess you've been there yourself. It was kind of eerie."

"Yes—it is." It was a small breathless voice now.

"So we went in there and I stuck a can up in a bull wheel for her to pop at. She threw a wingding. Looked like a mild epileptic fit to me."

"Yes." The same minute voice. "She has them once in a while. Is that all you wanted to see me about?"

"I guess you still wouldn't tell me what Eddie Mars has on you."

"Nothing at all. And I'm getting a little tired of that question," she said coldly.

"Do you know a man named Canino?"

She drew her fine black brows together in thought. "Vaguely. I seem to remember the name."

"Eddie Mars' triggerman. A tough hombre, they said. I guess he was. Without a little help from a lady I'd be where he is—in the morgue."

"The ladies seem to—" She stopped dead and whitened. "I can't joke about it," she said simply.

"I'm not joking, and if I seem to talk in circles,

it just seems that way. It all ties together—everything. Geiger and his cute little blackmail tricks, Brody and his pictures, Eddie Mars and his roulette tables, Canino and the girl Rusty Regan didn't run away with. It all ties together. . . ."

"You tire me," she said in a dead exhausted voice. "God, how you tire me."

"I'm sorry. I'm not just fooling around trying to be clever. Your father offered me a thousand dollars this morning to find Regan. That's a lot of money to me, but I can't do it."

Her mouth jumped open. Her breath was suddenly strained and harsh.

"Give me a cigarette," she said thickly. "Why?" The pulse in her throat had begun to throb. . . .

I stood up and took the smoking cigarette from between her fingers and killed it in an ashtray. Then I took Carmen's little gun out of my pocket and laid it carefully with exaggerated care, on her white satin knee. I balanced it there, and stepped back with my head on one side like a window-dresser getting the effect of a new twist of a scarf around a dummy's neck.

I sat down again. She didn't move. Her eyes came down millimeter by millimeter and looked at the gun.

"It's harmless," I said. "All five chambers empty. She fired them all. She fired them all at me."

The pulse jumped wildly in her throat. Her voice tried to say something and couldn't. She swallowed.

"From a distance of five or six feet," I said. "Cute little thing isn't she? Too bad I had loaded the gun with blanks." I grinned nastily. "I had a hunch about what she would do—if she got the chance."

She brought her voice back from a long way off. "You're a horrible man," she said. "Horrible."

"Yeah. You're her big sister. What are you going to do about it?"

"You can't prove a word of it."

"Can't prove what?"

"That she fired at you. You said you were down there around the wells with her alone. You can't prove a word of what you say."

"Oh that," I said. "I wasn't thinking of trying. I was thinking of another time—when the shells in the little gun had bullets in them."

Her eyes were pools of darkness, much emptier than darkness.

"I was thinking of the day Regan disappeared," I said. "Late in the afternoon. When he took her down to those old wells to teach her to shoot and put up a can somewhere and told her to pop at it and stood near her while she shot. And she didn't shoot at the can. She turned the gun and shot him, just the way she tried to shoot me today, and for the same reason."

She moved a little and the gun slid off her knee and fell to the floor. It was one of the loudest sounds I have ever heard. Her eyes were riveted on my face. Her voice was a stretched whisper of agony. "Carmen!—Merciful God, Carmen!—Why?"

"Do I really have to tell you why she shot at me?"

"Yes." Her eyes were still terrible. "I'm—I'm afraid you do."

"Night before last when I got home she was in my apartment. She'd kidded the manager into letting her in to wait for me. She was in my bed—naked. I threw her out on her ear. I guess maybe Regan did the same thing to her sometime. But you can't do that to Carmen."

She drew her lips back and made a halfhearted attempt to lick them.

It made her, for a brief instant, look like a frightened child. The lines of her cheeks sharpened and her hand went up slowly like an artificial hand worked by wires and its fingers closed slowly and stiffly around the white fur at her collar. They drew the fur tight against her throat. After that she just sat staring.

"Money," she croaked. "I suppose you want money."

"How much money?" I tried not to sneer.

"Fifteen thousand dollars."

I nodded. "That would be about right. That would be the established fee. That was what he had in his pockets when she shot him. That would be what Mr. Canino got for disposing of the body when you went to Eddie Mars for help. But that would be small change to what Eddie expects to collect one of these days, wouldn't it?"

She was as silent as a stone woman.

"All right," I went on heavily. "Will you take her away? Somewhere far off from here where they can handle her type, where they will keep guns and knives and fancy drinks away from her? Hell, she might even get herself cured, you know. It's been done."

She got up slowly and walked to the windows. The drapes lay in heavy ivory folds beside her feet. She stood among the folds and looked out toward the quiet darkish foothills. She stood motionless, almost blending into the drapes. Her hands hung loose at her sides. Utterly motionless hands. She turned and came back along the room and walked past me blindly. She was behind me when she caught her breath sharply and spoke.

"He's in the sump," she said. "A horrible decayed thing. I did it. I did just what you said. I went to Eddie Mars. She came home and told me about it, just like a child. She's not normal. I knew the police would get it all out of her. In a little while she would even brag about it. And if Dad knew, he would call them instantly and tell them the whole story. And sometime in that night he would die. It's not his dying—it's what he would be thinking just before he died. Rusty wasn't a bad fellow. I didn't love him. He was all right, I guess. He just didn't mean anything to me, one way or another, alive or dead, compared with keeping it from Dad."

"So you let her run around loose," I said, "getting into other jams."

"I was playing for time. Just for time. I played the wrong way, of course. I thought she might even forget it herself. I've heard they do forget what happens in those fits. Maybe she has forgotten it. I knew Eddie Mars would bleed me white, but I didn't care. I had to have help and I could only get it from somebody like him. There have been times when I hardly believed it all myself. And other times when I had to get drunk quickly—whatever time of day it was. Awfully damned quickly."

"You'll take her away," I said. "And do that awfully damned quickly."

She still had her back to me. She said softly now, "What about you?"

"Nothing about me. I'm leaving. I'll give you three days. If you're gone by then—okay. If you're not, out it comes. And don't think I don't mean that."

She turned suddenly. "I don't know what to say to you. I don't know how to begin . . ."

"Yeah. Get her out of here and see that she's watched every minute. Promise?"

"I promise . . ."

"Does Norris know?"

"He'll never tell."

"I thought he knew."

I went quickly away from her down the room and out and down the tiled staircase to the front hall. I didn't see anybody when I left. I found my hat alone this time. Outside, the bright gardens had a haunted look, as though small wild eyes were watching me from behind the bushes, as though the sunshine itself had something mysterious in its light. I got in my car and drove off down the hill.

What did it matter where you lay once you were dead? In a dirty sump or in a marble tower on top of a high hill. You were dead, you were sleeping the big sleep, you were not bothered by things like that. Oil and water were the same as wind and air to you. You just slept the big sleep, not caring about the nastiness of how you died or where you fell. Me, I was part of the nastiness now. Far more a part of it than Rusty Regan was. But the old man didn't have to be. He could lie quiet in his canopied bed, with his bloodless hands folded on the sheet, waiting. His heart was a brief uncertain murmur. His thoughts were as gray as ashes. And in a little while he too, like Rusty Regan, would be sleeping the big sleep. . . .

THE water looped out of the hose in a long lazy silver sluice as the Japanese gardener played it over the emerald lawn. The Sternwood house looked the same.

The general had died. Which was too bad. And Eddie Mars hadn't died, which was also too bad. And Carmen had been put away. But Vivian was still there. And Norris the butler was still there. He had called me and asked me to come out.

The place was full of remembrance. The same low solid foothills rose behind the house. The same terraced lawn dropped the long easy drop down to the barely visible oil derricks where a few barrels a day still creaked out of the ground. The sun shone on the olive trees and vivified the birds that fluttered among the leaves. The birds sang as if the world were still young.

Which it wasn't.

Norris answered my ring. He was tall and silver-haired, a vigorous sixty with the pink skin of a man who's circulation was good.

"Mr. Marlowe," he said. "Good of you to come."

The hallway was the same as it had been the first time I saw it. The portrait of the hot-eyed ancestor over the mantel. The knight and the lady forever still in the stained-glass window. The knight always trying to untie her. The lady always captive. The lady was still naked. The hair still conveniently long. It had been awhile since I had first stood here and Carmen Sternwood had told me I was tall and pitched into my arms. Only yesterday.

> She was twenty or so, small and delicately put together, but she looked durable. She wore pale blue slacks and they looked well on her. She walked as if she were floating. Her hair was a fine tawny wave cut much shorter than the current fashion of pageboy tresses curled in at the bottom. Her eyes were slate-gray, and had almost no expression when they looked at me. She came over near me and smiled with her mouth and she had little sharp predatory teeth, as white as fresh orange pith and as shiny as porcelain. They glistened between her thin too taut lips. Her face lacked color and didn't look too healthy.
>
> "Tall, aren't you?" she said.
>
> "I didn't mean to be."
>
> Her eyes rounded. She was puzzled. She was thinking. I could see, even on that short acquaintance, that thinking was always going to be a bother to her.

"Handsome too," she said. "And I bet you know it."

I grunted.

"What's your name?"

"Reilly," I said. "Doghouse Reilly."

"That's a funny name." She bit her lip and turned her head a little and looked at me along her eyes. Then she lowered her lashes until they almost cuddled her cheeks and slowly raised them again, like a theater curtain. I was to get to know that trick. That was supposed to make me roll over on my back with all four paws in the air.

"Are you a prizefighter?" she asked, when I didn't.

"Not exactly. I'm a sleuth."

"A—a—" She tossed her head angrily, and the rich color of it glistened in the rather dim light of the big hall. "You're making fun of me."

"Uh-uh."

"What?"

"Get on with you," I said. "You heard me."

"You didn't say anything. You're just a big tease." She put a thumb up and bit it. It was a curiously shaped thumb, thin and narrow like an extra finger, with no curve in the first joint. She bit it and sucked it slowly, turning it around in her mouth like a baby with a comforter.

"You're awfully tall," she said. Then she giggled with secret merriment. Then she turned her body slowly and lithely, without lifting her feet. Her hands dropped limp at her sides. She tilted herself toward me on her toes. She fell straight back into my arms. I had to catch her or let her crack her head on the tesselated floor. I caught her under her arms and she went rubber-legged on me instantly. I had to hold her close to hold her up. When her head was against my chest she screwed it around and giggled at me.

"You're cute," she giggled. "I'm cute too."

I didn't say anything. So the butler chose that convenient moment to come back through the French doors and see me holding her.

Well, maybe not quite yesterday.

I followed Norris's straight back down the same corridor toward the French doors. The house seemed quieter now. Probably my imagination. It was too big a house and too chilled with sadness ever to have been noisy. This time, we turned under the stairs and went down some stairs to the kitchen. The horsefaced maid was there. She smiled and bobbed her head at me. Norris glanced at her and she bobbed her head again and went out of the kitchen.

The kitchen was big and opened out onto the back lawn as it dropped away from the house. Like so many hillside mansions in Los Angeles the first floor in front was the second floor in back. The floors were a polished brown Mexican tile. There was a large wooden worktable in the center of the room, a big professional-looking cookstove against the far wall, two refrigerators to the right, and a long counter with two sinks and a set tub along the left wall.

"Will you have coffee, sir?" Norris said.

I said I would and Norris disappeared into a pantry off the kitchen and returned in a moment with a silver coffee service and a bone china cup and saucer. He poured the coffee into the cup in front of me. And placed an ashtray nearby.

"Please smoke if you wish to, Mr. Marlowe," Norris said.

I sipped the coffee, got out a cigarette and lit it with a kitchen match.

"How are the girls?" I said.

Norris smiled.

"The very subject I wished to discuss, sir."

Norris stood erect beside the table. I waited.

"The General used to like brandy in his coffee, sir," Norris said. "Would you care for some?"

"Join me," I said.

Norris started to shake his head.

"For the General," I said. Norris nodded, got another cup, put brandy in my cup and a splash, straight, in his cup.

He raised his cup toward me.

"To General Guy Sternwood," he said, giving "Guy" the French pronunciation.

I raised my cup back.

"General Sternwood," I said. I had first met him in the greenhouse, at the foot of the velvet lawn.

> The air was thick, wet, steamy and larded with the cloying smell of tropical orchids in bloom . . . after a while we came to a clearing in the middle

of the jungle, under the domed roof. Here, in a space of hexagonal flags, an old red Turkish rug was laid down and on the rug was a wheelchair, and in the wheelchair an old and obviously dying man watched us come with black eyes from which all fire had died long ago, but which still had the coal-black directness of the eyes in the portrait that hung over the mantel in the hall. The rest of his face was a leaden mask, with the bloodless lips and the sharp nose and the sunken temples and the outward-turning earlobes of approaching dissolution. His long narrow body was wrapped—in that heat—in a traveling rug and a faded red bathrobe. His thin claw-like hands were folded loosely on the rug, purple nailed. A few locks of dry white hair clung to his scalp, like wild flowers fighting for life on a bare rock.

I sipped my coffee. Norris took a discreet drink of his brandy. There was no sound in the big kitchen. The General's ghost was with us, and both of us were quiet in its presence.

"What do you know about my family?"

"I'm told you are a widower and have two young daughters, both pretty and both wild. One of them has been married three times, the last time to an ex-bootlegger who went in the trade by the name of Rusty Regan. That's all I heard, General. . . ."

"I'm afraid Miss Carmen has disappeared," Norris said, interrupting my thoughts.

"From where?" I said.

"After that, ah, misfortune with Rusty Regan," Norris said, "Miss Vivian placed her in a sanitarium as, I believe, you advised her to."

I nodded. The coffee was strong and too hot to drink except in small sips. The brandy lay atop the coffee and made a different kind of warmth when I sipped it. I could hear the General's voice thin with age, taut with feeling long denied.

> "Vivian is spoiled, exacting, smart, and quite ruthless. Carmen is a child who likes to pull wings off flies. Neither of them has any more moral sense than a cat. Neither have I. . . ."

There was another sound in the voice. Besides the tiredness and the iron self-control, there was a wistful sound, a sound of what might have been, a sound of sins revisited but irredeemable. And it was that sound which held me, as I knew it held Norris, if only in memory, long after the speaker had fallen silent.

> "Vivian went to good schools of the snob type and to college. Carmen went to half a dozen schools of greater and greater liberality, and ended up where she started. I presume they both had, and still have, all the usual vices. If I sound a little sinister as a parent, Mr. Marlowe, it is because my

hold on life is too slight to include any Victorian hypocrisy." He leaned his head back and closed his eyes, then opened them again suddenly. "I need not add that a man who indulges in parenthood for the first time at the age of fifty-four deserves all he gets. . . ."

"She was doing very well at the sanitarium," Norris said. "I myself had the privilege of visiting her every week."

"And Vivian?" I said. The daughters' names seemed to dispel the father's ghost.

"Miss Vivian visited whenever she was, ah, able." Norris turned the cup slowly in his clean strong hands. "Her father's death was difficult for her. And she is still seeing Mr. Mars."

Norris's voice was careful when he said it, empty of any evaluation. The voice of the perfect servant, not thinking, merely recording.

"How nice for her," I said. "Did she tell you to call me?"

"No, sir. I took that liberty. Miss Vivian feels that Mr. Mars will find Miss Carmen and return her to the sanitarium."

"His price will be higher than mine," I said.

"Exactly so, sir."

"And you know what I charge?"

"Yes, sir. You'll recall that I handled the General's checkbook for him when he employed you previously."

"And you can afford me?"

"The General was very generous to me in his will, sir."

I took a lungful of smoke and let it out slowly and tilted my chair on its back legs.

"But still you're working here," I said.

"I believe the General would have wished that, sir. His daughters . . ." Norris let the rest of the sentence disappear into an eloquent servant's self-effacement.

"Yes," I said. "I'm sure he would have. When did Carmen disappear?"

"A week ago. I went on my weekly visit and found that she was gone. The staff was somewhat reticent about her disappearance, but I was able to ascertain that she had in fact been gone for at least two nights."

"And no one had reported it?"

"Apparently not, sir. I informed Miss Vivian Sternwood, of course, and took the liberty of speaking on the telephone with Captain Gregory of the Missing Persons Bureau."

"And?" I said.

"And it was, as I remember his words, 'the first I'd heard of it.' "

"And Vivian?" I said.

"Miss Vivian said that I was not to worry about it. That she had resources and that Carmen would turn up."

"And by 'resources,' you understood her to mean Eddie Mars?" I said.

"I did, sir."

"How does she feel about you calling me?" I said.

"I have not yet informed her of that, sir."

I drank the rest of the coffee laced with brandy. It had cooled enough to go down softly. I nodded more to myself than to Norris.

"What is the name of this sanitarium?" I said.

"Resthaven, sir. It is supervised by a Dr. Bonsentir."

"Okay," I said, "I'll take a run out there."

"Yes, sir," Norris said. "Thank you very much, sir. May I give you a retainer?"

"A dollar will do for now," I said. "Make it official. We'll talk about the rest of it later."

"That's very kind indeed, sir," Norris said. He took a long pale leather wallet out of his inside pocket and extracted a dollar bill and gave it to me. I wrote him out a receipt, took the bill, and put it in my pocket, negligently, like there were many more in there and I had no need to think about it.

"May I call you here?" I said.

"Indeed, sir. I often receive calls here. Answering the phone is normally among my duties."

"And how is Vivian?" I said.

"She is still very beautiful, sir, if I may be so bold."

"And still dating a loonigan," I said.

"If you mean Mr. Mars, sir. I'm afraid that is the case."